FREE WILLY 3
THE RESCUE

Books by Todd Strasser

FREE WILLY 3
THE RESCUE

A novelization by Todd Strasser
Based on the screenplay written by John Mattson
and characters created by Keith A. Walker

© 1997 Warner Bros.

SCHOLASTIC INC.

New York   Toronto   London   Auckland   Sydney

ISBN 0-590-37403-6

12 11 10 9 8 7 6 5 4 3 2 1   7 8 9/9 0 1 2/0

Printed in the U.S.A.

First Scholastic printing, August 1997

To Emily, Dayna, and Nili Geldwert, who read like lightning and swim like fish.

FREE WILLY 3
THE RESCUE

1

A lot of being a kid is about killing time. Max Wesley knew that. He was ten, and he was killing time, waiting for the day when he could go out on his dad's boat. Waiting for the day when he would get his feet wet pulling in the nets and long lines filled with fish. Waiting for the day when he would finally be one of the crew.

Max raised the BB gun to his shoulder and aimed down the gun sight. His dad said he was too young to go out on a boat for weeks, and some times months at a time. He said Max was too small to handle the nets and the winches and the heavy-duty gear.

So Max had to kill time. At that moment he was doing it by killing *junk*. Lined up on the old wall twenty-five-feet away was the junk Max was killing that day — a plastic pig, a mug, a Coke can, a doll, a peanut-butter-and-jelly sandwich, and an apple.

Ping! Max hit the diving mask with a BB. He was disappointed with the result. He'd hoped to shatter it, but even though the glass was cracked, the BB still wasn't strong enough to do the job.

Next, Max aimed at the doll. *Plunk! Plunk! Plunk!* By rapidly firing he was able to knock it off the wall. Max smiled to himself. That was much more satisfying.

Next, he picked off the doll with one shot, then sank two shots into his peanut-butter-and-jelly sandwich.

Finally, Max aimed at the apple. This was the target he'd been waiting for. He always saved the best for last. His plan was to blow little bitelike chunks out of it until he worked his way right down to the core.

Max steadied the rifle and aimed just slightly off Apple Center. He was already smiling with anticipation as he started to squeeze the trigger . . .

Toooot! Somewhere in the distance, a boat whistle blew. Max jerked his head up. It sounded familiar. His dad had been out for nearly a month, and Max's mom said she expected him back any day now.

Maybe, just maybe, that was him.

2

Jesse was seventeen now, old enough to be legal in the banged-up VW van he was driving. He'd come a long way in the six years since he'd been a street urchin, living under bridges in the city and stealing food to survive. He had to admit that his foster parents, Annie and Glen, had done a pretty decent job of raising him. After all, if it weren't for them, he'd probably still be on the street or worse.

Instead, it was a warm sunny day and he was behind the wheel of his own van listening to tunes on the radio and free to go anywhere he pleased. Jesse glanced down at the radio and idly pushed the buttons, searching for a good song. On his third try he hit the Doobie Brothers' "China Grove," a very cool song he probably wouldn't even know about were it not for Glen.

Jesse started to sing along, tapping his left hand against the door. Suddenly through the noise of the traffic he thought he heard someone giggle. Looking at the car to his left, he came eye-to-eye with a smiling girl with long, shimmering reddish-brown hair.

It was obvious that she'd been listening to him sing along with the Doobie Brothers. Another guy might have been embarrassed, but Jesse just grinned back at her and started to sing even louder. The girl looked surprised for a moment, then gave him a warm, inviting gaze.

Jesse winked back. Traffic started to move and he punched the van into gear and glanced down at the duffle bag and laptop computer on the floor. On any other day he might have been more interested in the girl, but that day he had someplace else to go.

3

Max's bike banged down through the potholes filled with dirty water as he rode into the village. Ahead of him it spread out like a small crescent of buildings hugging the shore. Except he couldn't see any shore. Instead there were half a dozen creaking wooden docks lined with old, battered, weatherbeaten fishing boats.

Max rode his bike past the bank, the cafe where his mother worked, and the fish processing plant, then straight out onto one of the docks. Careful not to run over the water hoses, or into the lobster traps, he raced out to the slip of the *Botany Bay*, his dad's fishing boat.

Max stopped the bike. A tidal wave of disappointment washed over him. The slip was empty. The horn he'd heard before must've been from someone else's boat.

4

As he walked along the concrete piers with his duffle bag slung over his shoulder, Jesse fit the age-old image of a sailor getting ready to go sea. Only the laptop computer case in his hand seemed out of place.

He was looking for a ship. Not one of the fancy sailboats with the halyards clanging noisily against their forty-foot masts, nor one of the million-dollar yachts with their wave runners and satellite TVs. The boat he was looking for served a less frivolous purpose.

Jesse stopped. There she was, the *Noah*. From her high, pointed bow to her rounded aft, she was as sleek and polished a ship as he'd ever seen. Jesse felt his heart skip a beat as he eyed the radar and satellite dishes that adorned her bridge. If any boat could find a whale in an ocean, this was surely it.

"Hey, you," a voice said. Jesse turned. Behind

him on the pier was a kid carrying a couple of flat white pizza boxes. Emblazoned across the front of his shirt were the big red words PIZZA FACTORY. "That's twenty-two dollars, fifty cents."

Jesse shook his head. "I didn't order any pizzas."

The kid nodded at the ship. "That's the *Noah*, right?"

Jesse nodded.

"You on that boat?" the kid asked.

"I will be," Jesse answered.

The kid pushed the boxes toward him. "Then you ordered pizza."

Jesse dug into his pocket and came up with the money. He took the pizzas and crossed the metal gangplank and jumped onto the *Noah*'s deck. Out of the corner of his eye, he saw a woman coming toward him. She pulled the collar of her shirt toward her lips and said something he couldn't hear. As she got closer, he saw that she'd spoken into a small, clip-on microphone.

She stopped in front of Jesse and took the pizzas from him. "What do I owe you?"

"Twenty-two fifty," Jesse started to say. "But —"

She reached into her pocket, came up with a handful of bills, and handed them to him. "Here you go."

Jesse watched as she tore open the first box, pulled off a slice, and bit into it. She was older than him — maybe in her late twenties or early thirties — and awful pretty. He especially liked the way her greenish-blue eyes sparkled in the sunlight.

"You're not Drew, are you?" he asked.

She turned back to him and asked in a teasing way, "What if I am?"

"I'm Jesse," he said. "You hired me. Through Randolph."

At the sound of Randolph's name, the woman turned her lips down toward the collar mike again. "Hey, Randolph, you better hurry or you'll miss your pizza."

Now a big guy wearing a pressed white shirt and khakis joined them and took two slices at once. "So this is your secret," he said to the woman named Drew. "You hire crew from the Pizza Factory."

Then he turned to Jesse and offered a muscular hand. "I'm Stevens. First mate on this tub."

Jesse shook his hand. First mate Stevens took his slices and left. Jesse turned back to Drew, who was holding her slice in one hand and trying to open a Fed Ex package with the other.

"Listen," Jesse said, "I'm not from the Pizza Factory. I'm your research assistant."

Drew didn't look up from what she was doing. "What did you say your name was?"

"Jesse."

"Are you sure your name's not Willy?" she asked.

"Yeah, I'm positive." He couldn't tell if she was teasing him or not.

"That's funny," she said. "Because Randolph talked me into hiring a kid named Willy who he says has a knack for handling whales."

"Willy *is* a whale," Jesse tried to explain.

"No wonder he's good at it," Drew replied.

Jesse sighed and shook his head. He was pretty sure now that she was just giving him a hard time. Then Jesse's old friend Randolph leaned over the side of the bridge and waved to Jesse and Drew. Randolph, the Haida who, more than anyone else, had helped Jesse turn his life around. At that moment, Jesse was particularly glad to see him.

"Hey, Randolph," Jesse said, pointing at Drew. "Will you tell her who I am?"

"Never saw this kid before in my life." Randolph grabbed a slice and took a bite. "This is tasty pizza!"

Jesse rolled his eyes. It seemed like everyone on this ship was trying to be a comedian.

Meanwhile Drew turned to Randolph. "You didn't tell me he was so young."

"He's not so young," Randolph replied in a way that made Jesse certain he hadn't mentioned Jesse's age.

"Listen," Jesse butted in. "I'm just here to learn. I'll do everything you tell me."

Drew turned and studied him with a frown. "Everything?"

Jesse nodded.

Drew's frown turned into a smile. "I think we're going to get along fine."

5

Max sat hunched over on the couch in the den. In his hands was a game control. On the TV screen large green alien bug warriors were storming toward him.

Pow!Pow!Pow! Max mowed them down as easily as knocking junk off a wall. Somewhere behind him he heard the door open and knew his mom had come in from work. A moment later she put a plastic grocery bag on the floor and sat down next to him on the couch.

"Watch this," Max said. He switched from a machine gun to the hand grenade and threw it into the next wave of attackers. *Whomp!* The grenade went off, blowing away a whole bunch of them.

"You're getting pretty good at this," Mary Wesley said.

"Hang on," Max said, concentrating on yet another wave. "I have to kill fifty more."

"Fifty more what?" It was a typical Mom-type question.

"Bug warriors," Max said. "To get to the next level."

Mrs. Wesley reached into the grocery bag and came up with a colorful handful of Jolly Ranchers and an X-Men comic. Max quickly glanced at them, then mowed down a few more attackers.

"Thanks, Mom," he said.

Without asking, his mom unwrapped one of the Jolly Ranchers and slipped it into his mouth so he wouldn't have to take his hands off the game controls. All in all, it was a pretty cool move considering it was just before dinnertime.

"I talked to your father today on the ship-to-shore," she said. "It hasn't been going well. They're going to stay out a few more days."

Max nodded. It wasn't good news, but at least it was news he was used to.

"Know what else he said?" Mom asked.

Max shook his head and blasted a bug warship.

"He said maybe next time you could go with him."

Max straightened up and stared at her in disbelief. Go with Dad? On the *Botany Bay*?

"Would you like that?" Mrs. Wesley asked.

Max blinked. Was she *kidding*? On the TV screen there was some kind of commotion and a scream.

Mrs. Wesley gestured at the TV. "I think you died, Max."

But Max wasn't even thinking about the game anymore. "Dad really said that?"

"Yes, he did." Mrs. Wesley nodded and her forehead wrinkled a bit.

Max was puzzled. "What's wrong, Mom?"

She forced a smile on her face and rubbed his head affectionately. "Nothing, hon."

6

Randolph gave Jesse a tour of the *Noah*. The ship had been well maintained and outfitted with all the latest techno-gear for research.

Back on the deck, they met up with Drew again. Randolph, Jesse, and Drew sat down on the deck, and Randolph opened a case of small, red, electronic devices.

He picked one up and showed it to Jesse. "Ever see one of these before?"

Jesse shook his head no.

"It's a transmitter tag," Randolph said. "Tracking device. Instead of telling you where you're going by longitude and latitude, it tells you exactly where you are."

"I already know where I am," Jesse replied with a smile.

"But you don't know where the orcas are," Drew said. "The orca population has declined ten percent in the last two years. That's a pretty significant number, and we don't know why."

14

Randolph reached into the pelican case and came up with a dozen tubelike red tags. Each one had a thin wire with a barb on the end. Jesse immediately recognized them as the kind of tags environmentalists and scientists used to track fish.

"As you know, orcas travel in pods or families," Randolph said. "We're going to tag each pod with these. Then we'll be able to track those whales anywhere on the planet, twenty-four hours a day. It'll go a long way toward helping us figure out what's happening to them."

"What do you think is happening to them?" Jesse asked.

"Could be anything," Drew replied. "Environmental factors, a virus, old age. Ten percent is a pretty steep decline in a population, but for all we know it could be perfectly natural."

It didn't sound right to Jesse, and the grim look Randolph gave him confirmed that suspicion. Something was happening to the orcas, all right, and it was anything but "perfectly natural."

7

It was early morning and still dark out. Max stood in the front hall of his house waiting for his dad. He was wearing rubber boots, jeans, and a warm sweater under his jacket. At Max's feet was his overnight bag. In the bare yellow light, he was looking at some old framed photographs on the wall. In the photographs were men with moustaches or beards, holding long spears or knives on poles that looked like some kind of medieval weapon. Most of the men wore hats and long rubber boots. They were standing on something dark and rounded.

Only on closer inspection would you know that it was a whale.

Max always forgot exactly how he was related to the men in the photographs. But he never forgot that they were his ancestors, the whalers and fishermen who'd come before him and his dad.

"Ready?"

Max turned and saw his father, John Wesley,

16

smiling at him. He was not an old man, but his face was weathered and lined from a life at sea.

"You bet I am," Max said eagerly.

"Ready to catch some fish?" his father asked.

"Better believe it."

"Good." John Wesley patted his son on the shoulder. "This is a big day in your life. You're going out to sea."

The sky was just starting to turn the deep blue gray of predawn when they got down to the docks. Max and his father started down the creaking wooden dock, pausing briefly to say hello to the other fishermen preparing to go out in their boats.

Finally they got to the *Botany Bay*. Like the other fishing boats around her, the *Botany Bay* looked old and weatherbeaten, with gashes in her wooden hull and along her gunwale. Her bow was fortified with sections of old car tires, and more car tires served as fenders along her sides to keep her from banging into the sides of the slip. A rail made of gray pipe was the only thing on the deck for someone to hold on to. Forward of midships was the wheelhouse with its radar and radio towers perched above it. Behind the wheelhouse were the hoists and winches for laying out the nets, and the big drums upon which the nets were wrapped when not in use.

A dozen seagulls stood farther down the dock

and watched as Max and his father boarded the boat. Soon they would take flight and follow the fishing boat out to sea, always hoping to snag an easy meal when the nets were hauled.

Max stepped onto the wet deck of the *Botany Bay* and looked around in wonder. Of course, he'd been on the boat before, but never as a member of the crew. Down at the other end of the deck, three men were loading ice and supplies into the hold. When one of them, a tall man with brown hair and blue eyes who was wearing a heavy wool sweater, saw Max's father, he left the others and came forward.

"Captain." The man spoke with an accent and looked down at Max. Max stepped back, feeling uncertain under the man's intense gaze.

"This is my first mate, Hans Sanderson," John Wesley told his son. "Don't let him scare you."

"I won't." Max stepped forward.

"If he barks at you, just give it right back," his father said.

Sanderson reached forward and ruffled Max's hair. "What're you gonna be when you grow up, kid?"

"Your boss," Max replied with a grin.

Sanderson smiled back, then looked at Max's father. "Ready when you are, Captain."

"Good," John Wesley said. "I just want to show Max around and we'll be off."

Hans Sanderson went back to help the others,

and Max looked up at his father. "So, did I give it right back?"

"You sure did," his father replied. "Now let's get your gear stowed."

Max followed his father inside. His father's cabin was right behind the wheelhouse. It was small, with barely enough space for two berths, a table, and a chair. A single bare lightbulb hung from the ceiling above. Max stowed his bag in his berth, then noticed a sheathed knife lying on the table. The handle was the color of ivory. Max had never seen a handle like it before.

"That was my dad's knife," his father said behind him.

Max picked up the knife and gently slid it out of its sheath.

"It'll be yours someday," his father said.

"When?" Max asked. He slowly turned the knife in his hand. The blade glinted in the dull light.

"When you've earned it," John Wesley said. He took the knife from his son and slid it back into the sheath.

Max nodded, feeling disappointed, but also understanding. After all, he was still just a kid.

"I want you to have it," his father said. "And you will. When you're ready."

Max looked up at his father. "Will you show me how to use it?"

His father nodded with pride. "I'll show you everything I know, son."

8

The *Noah* was a dozen miles out to sea, with nothing but beautiful blue water and blue sky in every direction. But down in a windowless room below deck, Jesse was surrounded by tables full of the latest electronic gadgets and monitors. This was the ship's electronics room, the "brains" from where the sonar, radar, and hydrophone equipment was run.

At one table, Drew manned the sonar, the underwater radar that detected large objects like whales and schools of fish. At another table, Jesse had set up his laptop computer as well as a small electronic keyboard.

Drew peeled an orange and pretended to listen to the sonar, but Jesse knew she was watching him out of the corner of her eye. He was just about positive that she had no idea what he was doing, and he liked that idea that for once, *he* was teasing *her*. Of course, she must've sensed that, which was why she was trying so hard *not* to ask what he was up to.

Jesse reached into his pocket and took out a small microphone. He plugged its cord into the back of the laptop computer, then turned to Drew.

"Could you hold this please?" he asked, handing her the mike.

Drew took the mike, but her body language said she wasn't happy. Meanwhile, Jesse hit a couple of keys on the computer. The word "RECORDING" flashed in the upper left hand corner. Jesse took out his harmonica and played one long note into the mike Drew was holding.

That was the straw that broke the curious camel's back.

"What are you doing?" Drew asked.

Jesse smiled triumphantly as he took the microphone back. "Making a call."

Drew scowled, but didn't ask anything more. She popped a section of orange into her mouth. Jesse turned to the electronic keyboard and picked put a melody. It came out of the computer sounding like a harmonica. Next he turned to the laptop and pressed a few more keys. The harmonica melody played back again, and again. Jesse had turned it into an unending loop of music.

Drew crossed her arms and watched all this with a droll look on her face. Jesse decided he'd teased her enough. Now he owed her an explanation.

21

"Willy likes my harmonica playing," he said. "When he hears it, he knows it's me."

Drew nodded as if she now understood. "And you think you're going to play that sound over the hydrophone?"

"You got it," Jesse said.

"And Willy's going to come running from miles away?" Drew continued skeptically.

Jesse nodded and continued to type at the keyboard while the loop played over and over. "I'm changing the harmonica sample to fit Willy's ear. He has much better ears than we do and can hear —"

"Much higher sounds," Drew finished the sentence for him. "It's like a dog. See? I went to school too."

"I'm pitching the signal so high that we won't hear it." As Jesse spoke, the looping tune gradually disappeared. "Willy can still hear it. And now I can make it as loud as I want. If Willy's anywhere within thirty miles of us, he'll hear it."

Drew pressed a finger to her lips. "It's sort of like a Willy pager."

Jesse smiled proudly. "Pretty cool, huh?"

Drew tore off a section of the orange and handed it to him. "You thought of this yourself?"

"Yup."

She narrowed her eyes. "How old *are* you?"

"How old are *you*?" Jesse replied.

"That," Drew said, turning away, "is an awfully personal question."

9

The *Botany Bay* was also out at sea. While it looked like a very different boat from the *Noah* on the outside, it had a few surprising similarities inside. Like some very high-tech electronics.

"What is that?" Inside the wheelhouse, Max questioned a man named Kron who was wearing a pair of headphones and turning dials on a machine Max had never seen before. Max's dad was at the helm, steering the *Botany Bay*.

"Hydrophone," Kron replied. "You can hear things underwater."

"Like what?" Max asked.

"Whale calls for one thing," Kron said.

Max's dad turned from the wheel and looked at them. "Why don't you take the wheel, Kron," he said. "I want to take Max outside."

Max followed his dad outside. The *Botany Bay* cut smoothly through the gentle ocean rollers. Half a dozen seagulls glided hopefully behind the boat.

"How come she's called the *Botany Bay*, Dad?" Max asked.

"Well, I'm not really sure, son," John Wesley replied. "That was her name when I bought her. My understanding is that Botany Bay was where the British first landed when they claimed Australia as one of their colonies."

Max nodded, but he was now distracted by First Mate Sanderson, who came up through the fore hatch lugging a rusty metal thing that looked like a small cannon.

"Give me a hand, Captain?" Sanderson grunted, and Max's dad went to help. As they mounted the cannon on a post on the bow of the *Botany Bay*, Max realized that it was for shooting harpoons. Judging from the size of the harpoon, it must have been for really big fish. The thought excited Max.

"I have really good aim," he said.

Sanderson looked up from the cannon and gave him a wry smile. "At what?"

"Exterminator, Alien Invasion, Sea Creature, Wild West, Bug House . . ." Max rattled off the names of the video games he had mastered.

Sanderson looked back at Max's dad. "He probably *would* have good aim."

"Better believe it," John Wesley replied. "This kid's been doing target practice his whole life."

Suddenly, a horn above them sounded. Sanderson and Max's dad instantly became alert and scanned the sea around them. Max rushed to the pipe rail and peered out. Almost immediately he spied some black dorsal fins cutting through the water two hundred yards ahead.

"Dad!" He shouted excitedly and pointed. "Look!"

"I see them." John Wesley nodded calmly and positioned himself behind the harpoon cannon.

Max felt a jolt as the *Botany Bay* sped up and raced toward the group of black fins ahead. One of the fish blew a big spray of water into the air, and another poked his great black snout out of the water as if he was looking around. Max felt a shock of realization. He'd seen these creatures before . . . on TV and at the aquarium. These weren't fish, these were whales.

Why was his dad going after whales?

"Here, Max, hold this." His dad shook him from his thoughts as he handed him a long metal harpoon with a rope attached to one end.

"What do I do?" Max asked.

"Help me reload," his father said. "Just give it to me when I tell you."

Max nodded. No, he decided, they *couldn't* be after the whales. They must've been going after whatever the whales were chasing. Yes, he thought, that had to be it. They followed the whales because the whales knew where the fish were.

The boat was closing fast on the whales. Max's dad stayed behind the harpoon cannon, aiming intently down the barrel. Sanderson was standing beside him, focused on the scene ahead.

Max pressed his hands against the pipe rail. The whales were like fat black torpedoes swimming just beneath the surface ahead of the *Botany Bay*. As the ship caught up to them, one black shape veered off away from the others.

"Now!" Sanderson shouted.

"Not yet," Max's dad replied calmly, aiming the cannon. "Not just yet . . ."

Boom! The report of the cannon caught Max by surprise. He spun around and stared at the barrel as a puff of smoke rose and disappeared into the breeze. His father's face, and the faces of the others started to fill with elation.

"You got him!" Sanderson shouted.

Max quickly pressed himself against the pipe rail and looked down into the water, but the black shape had vanished.

Got what? Max wondered.

"Pull around!" his father shouted. "Hard port!"

The *Botany Bay* veered around so sharply that Max almost lost his grip on the rail. He could see more black shapes ahead in the water.

"Now, Max!" a voice shouted. But the words meant nothing to Max.

"Max!" the voice shouted more insistently. *"Now!"*

That snapped Max out of his daze. The next

thing he knew, his father snatched the second harpoon out of his hands and jammed it into the cannon.

The black shapes were off to the left now, picking up speed.

Boom! The cannon fired again. Max watched the harpoon slice through the water, just barely missing one of the black shapes. Behind him, his father grunted and grabbed another weapon. This one looked like a rifle with a thinner, but no less lethal-looking, spear sticking out of it.

"There's one!" Sanderson shouted, pivoting to the right.

John Wesley wheeled around, aimed, and fired. *Bang!* The spear rocketed into the water, hitting one of the whales in the tail. The creature shivered momentarily, then disappeared below the surface of the water.

For a moment, everything went silent. The *Botany Bay* shut down its engine and sat.

"He'll be back up," Max's father said, loading another one of the big harpoons into the cannon.

They waited in silence, everyone pressed to the rail, looking out over the ocean around them. Max found himself wishing — *praying* — the whale wouldn't come up. He picked up a pair of binoculars and focused them on the broad smooth waves.

Then, out in the distance, a black dorsal fin broke the surface. It was different from the other ones, curled over instead of straight and pointy. Max lowered the binoculars. What if he asked his father to let that one go?

"Dad?" he began.

John Wesley's reaction was far swifter than Max expected. He looked exactly where Max had been looking. "There he is! Good eyes, Max!"

Before Max could say another word, his father shouted, "Hard port!" and the chase began again. The *Botany Bay* roared back to life and lurched to the left. Once again Max had to grab the rail to keep from falling. His father took his position behind the harpoon cannon. Seeing him there made Max realize how hopeless it was. There was no way he was going to talk his father out of harpooning that whale now.

Max turned and looked ahead, hoping the whale would dive again. Instead, the whale was heading straight for them! The curled dorsal cut through the water on a collision course with the *Botany Bay*! Max couldn't believe it. Was that whale crazy or what?

"Darn!" his father muttered. Max saw that he couldn't get a shot at the whale straight over the bow. The very front of the boat was just a little too high. Max looked back down at the whale swimming toward them. *Did he know that? Could he be that smart?*

"Starboard!" John Wesley shouted. "Now!"

The boat heaved to the right. Max tumbled backward. He felt his momentum carry him right over the ship's gunwale. He reached out for the rail, but this time he missed.

The next thing Max knew, he was falling.

10

Jesse stood on the deck of the *Noah* scanning the water with his binoculars. They were an old pair. He'd had them since he was twelve. But it didn't matter. Once Willy heard that synthesized call from the hydrophone, Jesse was confident that he'd come no matter what.

"Any luck yet?" It was Drew, coming toward him on the deck.

"Not yet," Jesse replied. He still wasn't sure what he thought about her. He sort of liked her teasing sense of humor, but he couldn't tell if she really liked him or was just goofing on him.

"I feel like I might have come on a little strong before, down in The Pit," she said. "I just want you to know I didn't mean anything by it. That idea you had for the hydrophone was pretty impressive."

Jesse nodded. "Don't worry about it. I didn't notice." But of course he had, and now he felt much better. She was apologizing. She wouldn't have done that if she didn't like him.

She handed him another pair of binoculars. "Try these. I think you'll see farther."

Jesse pressed them to his eyes. She was right. They were much clearer and stronger. "Hey, thanks."

"No sweat." Drew patted him on the back and left.

Jesse scanned the waves back and forth in a 180-degree sweep. The *Noah* was barely skirting the edge of the world's largest ocean. Willy could have been a thousand miles away. But in his gut, Jesse knew he was closer. A *lot* closer.

Now someone else sidled up to him. Jesse turned and looked into the weatherbeaten face of Randolph.

His good friend frowned.

"What's wrong?" Jesse asked.

"Uh, nothing." Randolph shook his head and stared at Jesse's face.

"Let me guess," Jesse said. "I've got a monster zit?"

"No, no." Randolph shook his head and gazed out at the ocean.

"Okay, everyone," a voice called behind them. Jesse turned to find Drew, First Mate Stevens, and Captain Drake. Drake was shorter and more compactly built than Stevens, but just as stiffly starched. He was holding a Polaroid camera.

"What's going on?" Jesse asked as Randolph, Stevens, and Drew crowded around him.

"Just a little tradition, kid," Captain Drake replied. "Group portrait whenever we set sail."

Everyone around Jesse seemed to think that was as funny as anything, but he didn't see what all the smirking was about.

"Big smiles, everyone," Captain Drake said, and aimed the camera. He took a shot, then made them hang around for another.

"Welcome aboard, kid," Drake said, handing the camera to Drew and shaking Jesse's hand. The others left, chuckling. Jesse still couldn't figure out what was so funny.

Drew pulled the film out of the camera and handed it to Jesse. It was still in the process of developing.

"I think you're going to like it," she said with a broad smile. "It brings out your eyes."

She left him alone and went below deck. Jesse stood there staring down at the photograph.

It slowly developed.

But there was something wrong. Jesse saw that his eyes were all black, like a raccoon.

The photo grew clearer still. Jesse squinted and gritted his teeth. He raised a finger to his eyes and rubbed. The finger came away black with soot.

Soot from the kerosene heater in the galley that

Drew must've put on the binoculars before she gave them to him.

So it brought out his eyes, huh? Jesse shook his head angrily and headed below deck to wash his face. He'd show Drew that two could play this game.

11

Max stood in his father's cabin, absent-mindedly buttoning a dry shirt. His thoughts went back to what had happened earlier. Back to that moment after he hit the water and went under.

How he'd opened his eyes and everything around him was green.

How cold the water was as it went through his clothes and hit his skin.

But mostly how the whale with the curled dorsal fin had come right toward him, and for an instant Max had imagined that it was going to eat him. And that maybe he deserved it for being on the boat that had hurt the whale and his friends.

Instead the whale had passed by so close that Max could have reached out and touched him. And even in the blur of the water, Max could see the whale's great brown eye looking at him.

And then the whale was gone and Max realized he couldn't breathe. He'd kicked and thrashed his way back to the surface where his father had reached under the pipe rail and yanked him out of the water by his arms.

Max had expected his father to be angry, but John Wesley wasn't. Instead he looked upset, and even scared, as if he was thinking of how close his son had come to drowning.

He'd brought Max down to the cabin to change out of his wet clothes. As Max changed, he considered what would take place if his dad's crew killed a whale.

And Max knew what would happen next because he'd seen the pictures at home. He knew how the whale's blubber and fat would be stripped away, and the meat sliced. And how every piece would be put on ice and saved. His father had told him that in the old days, when you killed a whale, you used every single part of it. But Max thought that was only in the old days. He didn't know his father was killing whales.

Max tucked the dry shirt into his pants.

Rap! Rap! There was a knock on the door, and his dad stuck his head in. "Dinner's served."

Max nodded silently and followed him down the narrow hallway and into the little galley where the crew sat pressed closely together around a small table. They made a space for him and Max sat down.

"First day, Max, congratulations." The man named Kron gave him a pat on the back.

"I didn't do anything," Max replied with a shrug.

"On this boat we work together," said a man named Dineen. "Everyone shares the credit."

"That's . . . great," Max said, forcing a small smile onto his lips. How could he explain that he *didn't* want to share the credit. Not for killing whales . . .

Sanderson dug into his pocket and handed him something. It was a rope necklace and hanging from it was what looked like a spear tip made of ivory.

"Carved from the tooth of a sperm whale," Sanderson said. "Souvenir from our last trip."

"You're one of us," added Kron.

Max nodded and said thanks. So it wasn't unusual for his father to hunt whales. The truth was, Max had sensed that the first time he saw the harpoon cannon. It was simply too big for any fish the regular fishermen brought into the processing plant. Max didn't know all the laws, but he was pretty darn sure people weren't supposed to hunt whales anymore.

And if that was correct, it meant his father was breaking the law.

Later, Max went out on the deck. The sky was clear, the blackness awash with stars. The only way he could tell where the sky ended and the ocean began was by where the stars stopped. The inky darkness of the ocean spread away in every direction. Max wondered how far away from land they were. The thought made him feel a little jittery, but that was okay.

What wasn't okay was the way he felt about his dad, and what his dad was doing. Was it possible that he, Max, was wrong? That somehow it was okay for his dad to hunt whales? If not, why did his dad do it? Why didn't he catch salmon and halibut and sardines like the other fishermen from their village?

Max leaned against the pipe rail. With his feet he absent-mindedly kicked at a tire that was being used as a bumper on the boat. It made a small, high-pitched squeak.

Squeak . . .

Max's head popped up. Was it his imagination or did something, or someone, squeak back?

He peered into the darkness, but saw nothing. Max moved the tire back and forth again. *Squeak.*

Squeak . . .

There it was again. Something was definitely answering him. He moved the tire a longer distance. *Squeeeeeak* . . .

Squeeeeeak . . . Came the reply.

Max pressed against the rail and stared into the water. What was it? *Where* was it?

A movement just below the surface startled him. It was that whale! Right there beside the boat, but in the darkness, almost invisible. Max saw a glint deeper in the water. The thin spear his father had shot was still stuck in the whale's tail. The thought made him wince. It must've hurt. He remembered reading in school that whales were warm-blooded mammals like dogs and horses and human beings.

Why was this whale hanging around the *Botany Bay*? Didn't he know that was dangerous?

Squeak. Max heard another squeak, but knew that one wasn't from the whale. It came from a hatch. Someone was coming onto the deck. He quickly leaned down toward the whale and hissed, "Go on! Get out of here! They'll kill you!"

The darn whale didn't move. He just floated there beside the boat looking up at him. Meanwhile, whoever had come through the hatch was coming closer. In desperation, Max picked up a plastic float and threw it at the whale.

With a soft *plup!* the whale sank below the surface and disappeared. Max breathed a sigh of relief and turned to greet whoever was coming.

Thunk! The next thing he knew, the float landed at his feet. Max stared back down at the water in amazement. The whale had thrown it back at him!

Max quickly picked up the float. At the same time, a silhouette appeared on the deck. Max recognized it at once. It was his dad.

"Hi, Dad," Max said, holding the float awkwardly.

His father didn't answer. Instead he peered out at the inky water. "Hear that?"

"Hear what?" Max asked, hoping his dad wasn't referring to the whale.

"Listen," John Wesley said softly.

Max didn't want to listen. He didn't want to hear that that whale was still hanging around. "What, Dad?"

"They make this sound," His father pursed his lips and blew some air out. "The sound of their blowhole. I thought I heard it."

"I didn't hear anything," Max said, praying the whale would just *go away.*

John Wesley scanned the water again, then spoke in a low, controlled voice. "Get me my spear gun."

Max took a step back. He didn't want to get the spear gun. He didn't want to do anything to hurt that whale. But this was his father, and he always did what his father said.

John Wesley glanced at his son and was a little surprised to see him still standing there on the deck. "Quietly, now," he said. "Go."

Max turned toward the bow. How could he not do what his father ordered? First, he was his father. Second, he was captain of the ship. You always did what the captain ordered, always. It was in Max's blood. He was a Wesley, and as far back as anyone could remember, Wesleys had gone to sea and obeyed their captains.

Max went to the locker on the deck where the spear guns were stowed. He opened it and hesitated. Inside were guns that were made to kill living things that shouldn't be killed.

"Max, hurry!" Down the deck his father hissed. "I see him."

Max felt his heart sink. Now what? How could he possibly obey his father and at the same time keep him from killing the whale? He didn't have the answer as he picked up a spear gun and started back toward his father. But ahead of him on the deck was a gear box and suddenly Max had the solution.

Max ran right into the box, intentionally tripping himself. *Ooofff!* The spear gun flew out of his hands and clattered noisily on the deck.

Max curled up on the deck and grabbed his shin, which throbbed painfully. He truly hoped he'd scared the whale away because he'd really done a number on his shin.

He had hoped the clamor would alert the whale to the danger, but he hadn't realized that the noise would bring the rest of the *Botany Bay*'s crew running. Overhead lights flashed on all over the boat and men with spear guns started firing.

Max winced. What if it hadn't worked? What if he'd made the dumbest mistake ever? Now, instead of just his father, they were all firing at the whale. Max struggled to his feet just in time to see four spears arc through the air and splash into the water. John Wesley stood frozen at the rail, watching.

"Did you get him, Dad?" Max asked, praying the answer would be no.

John Wesley didn't answer. It was a little spooky, how he just stood there and stared out into the dark.

"Dad?" Max repeated nervously. Was his father incredibly mad at him for tripping and making all that noise?

John Wesley blinked and looked at Max. His eyes traveled down to the boy's shin. Max looked down and saw a red spot the size of a half dollar spreading through the material of his pants.

"You cut your shin," John Wesley said. "We better take care of that."

They went down to his father's cabin. John Wesley opened a first-aid kit and took out some gauze and tape. Max watched as his father expertly dressed the wound. Now he felt bad.

"I'm sorry I screwed up, Dad."

"You'll be okay," his father replied. "After you get your first."

"My first?" Max didn't know what his father was talking about.

"Your first kill," his father said.

Max averted his eyes. Kill? How could he kill a whale? How had he gotten himself into this mess?

41

His father patted him on the shoulder. "Did I ever tell you about when I got my arm caught in the whale line, with a harpooned Right whale on the other end?"

Max shook his head.

"I'll never make that mistake again," his father said. "That's what mistakes are for. You learn."

Max looked up at his father. He didn't want to learn. He didn't want to kill. But his father misread his expression.

"Hey," John Wesley said with a smile, touching his son's shin. "You might even get a little scar here if you're lucky. Now maybe you ought to get some sleep."

Lucky? Max thought ruefully. Right now he felt like about the most *un*lucky kid alive. His father stood up and started toward the door.

But before he left, there was something Max needed to know.

"Dad?"

John Wesley turned. "Yes?"

"How did you know the whale was there?"

"You get a sense," his father answered. "You'll get it, too, after a while. Never take your eye off the ball, Max. If you do, either the sea will get you, or a whale will."

Max grimaced. His father must've thought he was upset because he said, "Don't worry, son. We'll get him first. I promise."

*　　*　　*

Later, Max lay in his bed in the dark, running his fingers over the whale's tooth necklace. Tears fell out of his eyes. All he'd ever wanted was to go out with his father on the *Botany Bay*.

Now he wished he'd never come.

12

Lying in his bed on the *Noah* not that many miles away, Jesse also ran his fingers over a carving. It was a small wooden carving of an orca that Randolph, who was snoring away in the bunk below him, gave him one night five years before. It was a night Jesse would never remember. He'd snuck into the aquarium to say good-bye to Willy because he was going to run away. He'd slipped, banged his head, and fallen unconscious into the tank where Willy was held. He would have drowned if Willy hadn't saved him.

Jesse felt his eyelids grow heavy and knew he'd be asleep soon. It was kind of neat that he could fall asleep while the ship's hydrophone continued to broadcast its call to Willy. Jesse closed his eyes. The *Noah*'s hydrophone could only reach thirty miles away, but Willy could have been a thousand miles away. But Jesse knew his orca friend was closer. He could *feel* it.

*   *   *

44

Thump. Jesse rolled over and tucked his pillow under his head.

Thump. He rolled onto his back.

Thump. He just couldn't find a comfortable position. He opened his eyes. Sunlight filtered into the cabin he shared with Randolph.

Thump. Jesse frowned as he realized that something was thumping against the hull of the *Noah*. Was it a log, or ... He sat up and smiled. *Of course!*

In a flash he hopped out of bed and pulled on his clothes. A second later he was racing up the metal ladder toward the deck. The deck was slick with early morning dew and a mist hung over the smooth waters. Jesse pressed himself against the *Noah*'s gunwale and looked over the side. There was Willy, spyhopping.

"Hey, boy!" A smile spread over Jesse's face. "What took you so long?"

Willy responded with a high-pitched, anxious sound. Jesse's smile instantly disappeared. Something was wrong. He hadn't heard that cry since he and Willy had been trapped beneath a burning oil slick several years before.

"Just stay there," Jesse said. He went down the deck to a rope ladder that hung over the side of the hull. Jesse quickly climbed down toward the water. When he got close, he reached out to pet Willy's snout.

"What is it, Willy?" he asked. "What's wrong?"

Willy made that distressed cry again, then sank beneath the surface. Jesse looked up the hull. Now Randolph was up there, looking down at him. Jesse could see concern in his own friend's face.

"What's wrong?" Randolph asked.

"I don't know," Jesse replied. "But something's happened. Willy's pretty freaked."

They needed permission from Captain Drake to take out the dinghy, a white rubber boat with a small outboard engine, to take a closer look at Willy. When they got into it, Jesse noticed that Randolph was wearing his collar mike and earphones.

"What's the point?" Jesse asked as he started up the outboard and steered toward the cove where Willy was circling in an agitated manner.

"Sometimes it's good to stay in touch," Randolph replied, jerking his head back at the *Noah*.

Jesse looked back. Drew was on the deck, watching them. Captain Drake was standing next to her. From the expressions on their faces it looked like they were having a serious conversation.

"You're listening in?" Jesse asked Randolph.

Randolph nodded. "Drake wants to know how long this is going to take. Drew is telling him she doesn't know. Now Drake's saying he isn't comfortable anchored here. He's worried the wind may kick up."

Jesse looked up at the tall spruces lining the

cove. The tops of the trees were perfectly still. Jesse had a feeling the wind wasn't going to kick up anytime soon. But Drake was the type who didn't go by feelings. He went by numbers.

"Drew just asked if we could have a day," Randolph reported. "Drake reminded her that she had twelve pods of orcas to tag and not a whole lot of time to do it. He's wondering why we'd want to spend so much time on a stray."

"Because it's Willy, that's why," Jesse replied.

Randolph pointed at his collar mike and smiled. "Want to tell the captain that?"

Jesse shook his head. Drake wouldn't understand.

"Okay," Randolph said. "Drew just told Drake to leave everything to her, and just let her know if and when they fall behind schedule."

Up on deck, Captain Drake turned away. Drew spoke into her collar mike. "You hear that?"

"The captain is very helpful, isn't he?" Randolph replied into his collar mike with more than a little sarcasm.

"They didn't hire him to be helpful," Drew replied dryly. "They hired him to protect their big expensive boat."

"I'll keep that in mind," Randolph said.

"You'll get used to him," Drew said about Captain Drake. "As long as we're on schedule and keep the boat clean, he won't bother us."

Jesse and Randolph were almost to the cove

now. Willy came out and started to swim alongside the dinghy. Jesse saw a glint of metal near his tail. His jaw dropped when he realized that something long and shiny was sticking out of it.

"Randolph, look!" he pointed. "What is that?"

Randolph leaned over the side of the dinghy. Jesse watched the expression on his friend's face change. His forehead bunched up and the corners of his mouth turned down.

"Is it a spear?" Jesse asked.

"Yes," Randolph replied gravely.

Jesse stared at Willy's tail in astonishment and anger. It was totally against the law. Worse than that, it was wrong.

"Jesse," Randolph had caution in his voice.

A ten percent drop in the orca population in the past two years, Jesse thought, clenching his fist. No wonder . . .

"Jesse," Randolph said again.

Jesse slowly turned to his friend. A seething anger boiled inside him. "Whalers did this."

Randolph nodded. It was just as he'd feared.

13

Max stood with his father in the wheelhouse of the *Botany Bay*. After a night's rest, things were a little better. At least he didn't feel so upset. Maybe they'd get lucky. Maybe they wouldn't see another whale for the rest of the trip.

The wheelhouse door opened and the man named Kron came in carrying a reel of tape. "I've got something I think you should hear," he said to Max's father.

John Wesley nodded to an old reel-to-reel tape recorder, and Kron started to run the tape through the heads. "I recorded this last night," Kron explained. "I wouldn't have even *known* about it if it wasn't for the readouts I saw on the hydrophone screen. Whatever this is, it's way above what a human can hear."

Max's father raised a curious eyebrow and glanced at his son. "This should be interesting," he said. "I've been going out to sea my whole life and this is a first."

"For me, too," Kron said, still setting up the tape. "I wanted to hear what it would sound like to us, so I brought it down a few hundred octaves."

John Wesley looked up. "You said a few *hundred*?"

"That's right," Kron said. "And this is what I got."

He pressed play and a strange sound started playing. To Max, it sounded a little like a harmonica.

"That's no animal I've ever heard," his father said.

"You're right about that," Kron agreed. "It's not an animal. It's a loop. It plays over and over again. I've been picking it up now for the past eighteen hours."

John Wesley and Kron shared a puzzled look.

"What is it?" Max's father asked.

"And where's it coming from?" Kron asked back.

14

Jesse stroked Willy's snout, trying to soothe him.

"Come on, Willy," Jesse said gently. "We're just trying to help you."

Willy grew calmer in the water. Randolph reached over the side of the dinghy and slowly tried to grab the thin metal spear stuck in the orca's tail.

Ker-splash! Willy thrashed his tail so hard he knocked the dinghy half a dozen feet away. Jesse and Randolph held onto the side of the rubber raft. Water dripped down their faces as they watched Willy swim away.

"You okay?" Jesse asked.

"Yeah." Randolph nodded. "Guess Willy's pretty upset."

"I would be too," Jesse replied. "If someone shot me with a spear."

Fuff! Deeper in the cove, Willy breached, sending a spout of vapor into the air.

Jesse raised a pair of binoculars and scanned the waters. "I wonder where the rest of the pod is."

"We have to get that spear out before an infection sets in," Randolph said.

In the cove, Willy let out a wailing call.

"He's calling to the rest of the pod," Jesse said. "Maybe if we could get him back to them, he'd calm down a little."

"Got any suggestions on how to do that?" Randolph asked.

Jesse pressed his lips together and thought. "Yeah, I have a suggestion. Let's go back to the *Noah.*"

A little while later, in The Pit and surrounded by electronic equipment, Jesse plugged one end of a long, thin cable into the hydrophone console. Then he started unrolling the cable out of The Pit, up the metal stairs and out onto the deck where Randolph waited, holding a shotgun mike poking out of the middle of a clear plastic dish.

"I feel like I'm on the sidelines at a football game," Randolph quipped as Jesse came toward him with a cable.

Nearby, Drew leaned against the gunwale, watching Willy as he circled the cove and let out his keening wail again.

"What's Willy doing?" Drew asked.

"He's calling his family," Randolph replied.

"But they'll never hear him," Drew said.

Jesse plugged the end of the cable into the shotgun mike. "They'll hear him now."

15

The *Botany Bay* moved along at a steady pace. Max's father was in the wheelhouse. Kron and Dineen were on deck, scanning the horizon for sign of a whale. Max stood at the rail, watching a couple of dolphins cavort in the boat's wake. His father and the others ignored the dolphins. Max assumed there wasn't enough meat on them to make it worth their while.

Thank God.

A high-pitched scraping sound caught Max's attention. It seemed to be coming from below decks. Having nothing better to do, Max followed it to a hatch door that was slightly ajar. A light was on inside. Max opened the hatch and lowered himself inside.

He was shocked at what he'd walked into. It was a small room, but it might have been a medieval storage room for weapons. Max was surrounded by harpoons, spears, cross-bows, and flensing knives that resembled battle-axes.

Seated in the middle of it all was Sanderson, sharpening blades on a small electric grinding wheel. He watched as Max stopped and studied the tip of an exploding harpoon.

"Look, but don't touch," the first mate warned him.

"What is it?" Max asked.

"Exploding harpoon," Sanderson replied matter-of-factly. "The tip pierces the whale's skin, then explodes. We use it on the bigger ones."

Max felt a chill run down his arms. "Then what?"

"Slice them into sections," the first mate explained. "Harvest the meat. Freeze for shipping." He swiveled around in his chair and opened a freezer door. Inside were long frozen strips of flesh, like reddish wooden logs.

Max felt ill, but tried not to show it. Sanderson slammed the freezer door shut. "Next time we get a whale, I'll show you how to flense it if you want."

Max couldn't imagine anything he'd want to do less. "So, uh, who do you sell it to?"

"Norway, Russia, Japan," Sanderson replied offhandedly. "Anyone who pays. Believe it or not, there's a big market for whale meat."

There were still things Max wasn't completely sure about. He decided to play dumb in order to find out. "I never see it for sale in the fish market."

Sanderson grinned. "It's an underground market."

"You mean, illegal?" Max said.

Sanderson leveled his gaze at him. "They're paying about eighty cents a pound for halibut, kid. Know what *one* pound of whale meat will earn you?"

Max shook his head.

Sanderson nodded. *"Two hundred dollars."*

16

Once Jesse had Willy's call on tape, he made a loop and cranked it up as high as it would go on the hydrophone. In The Pit he joked about playing "Willy karaoke," while on deck the rest of the crew wore earplugs to muffle the repeated cry.

The day passed into night. Bundled under a blanket, Jesse maintained his lonely vigil until he fell asleep.

Jesse opened his eyes. Above him the sky was gray, and slightly reddish to the east. The air was cold and misty. It was morning and he'd slept all night on the deck. He uncurled his legs and stretched them. He felt stiff.

Snorrrrt . . . He heard an unfamiliar sound. Standing up, he looked out into the cove. At first there was nothing but flat, glassy water. Then all of a sudden, four large black backs broke the surface in unison.

Snorrrrt . . . They exhaled together, then sank

57

again out of sight. Jesse watched, fascinated. He'd never seen a pod of orcas sleep before, but that was clearly what they were doing. Rising, breathing, sinking, and probably dreaming of juicy king salmon for breakfast.

Jesse heard a squeak and turned to see a hatch open. Randolph came out yawning and joined him at the gunwale. Jesse smiled at him. "I can't believe our Willy karaoke actually worked."

Randolph nodded and gazed out at the sleeping whales.

Snorrrrt . . .

"Willy snores," Jesse said.

"So do you," Randolph replied.

Jesse was surprised. "But I don't sound like that."

Randolph raised an eyebrow.

Jesse couldn't believe it. "Do I?"

His friend patted him on the back. "It's okay, Jesse."

17

Max's father wanted to show him how to use the harpoon cannon. Max knew he'd have to pretend to be interested. It was his way of surviving. All he wanted was to get through this trip. Things would be better once he had dry land under his feet again.

He stood on the fore deck while his father pulled the tarp off the cannon. Their eyes met. His father smiled. "You being here means a lot to me, Max."

Max nodded, but had to avert his eyes. "Me, too, Dad."

His father gestured to the cannon. "Get behind her and I'll show you."

Max stood behind the harpoon cannon. The metal was cold and damp to the touch. *How many whales had his father murdered with it?* Max shook his head. He had to stop thinking like that. He felt his father's hands on his shoulders, slowly moving him from left to right.

"Remember you'll be aiming at something that's

moving," John Wesley was saying. "You'll be moving too. You have to picture where the target is going to be and aim there."

Never, Max thought.

"It's like throwing a football on the run," his father went on. "It happens too fast to think about it much. You just have to feel it."

"It's just like playing catch," Max repeated mechanically. Actually, it was *nothing* like playing catch.

"That's right," his father said.

"I just have to feel it," Max said. "And kind of . . . not think." *Fat chance.*

"You'll get the hang of it." John Wesley patted his son on the shoulder and sounded just like the loving father he was. "It won't take you long."

18

Jesse had put on a wet suit, snorkel, and mask. He loved snorkeling. It was as close to being a whale as a human could get. And right now he was pretty close to a whale. He was swimming under Willy's tail with a pair of cable cutters.

From underneath, he could see that the head of the spear had gone straight through the tail. That was good news, actually. Jesse got the cable cutters around the shaft of the spear just below the head and squeezed hard. The cutters closed and the spear tip was severed. Jesse grabbed it. Next, he swam around and grabbed the shaft of the spear. With one tug he was able to pull it free.

With the spear removed, Willy immediately swam off. Jesse rose to the surface and snorkeled back to the dinghy where Drew and Randolph helped him aboard.

"Get the spear?" Randolph asked.

"Got it," Jesse said. He pulled off his mask and watched as Willy playfully bumped noses with another orca. "Who's the whale with Willy? It looks like they know each other."

"That's Nicky," Randolph said.

The two whales swam close together, corkscrewing around each other.

"Is that a boy Nicky, or a girl Nicky?" Jesse asked.

"She's a girl," Randolph replied.

Jesse made a fist and grinned. "Way to go, Willy!"

Randolph took out one of the transmitter tags. When he activated the tag, a small blip appeared on Drew's laptop screen. Jesse knew what that meant and turned to the whales.

"Yo, Willy!" he called. "Come on, boy, time to hook up. Hey, I know you're busy, but this is important."

But Willy ignored him and kept playing.

"Guess they have better things to do," Drew said with a shrug.

"I think I can get their attention," Randolph said, opening his bag and pulling out a bag of oranges.

"Oh, Randolph, you shouldn't have," Drew said and reached for one.

But Randolph held them out of her reach. "I didn't."

The corners of Drew's mouth turned down. "Then, you should have."

"They're not for you," Randolph said, and

heaved an orange toward the whales. "I spent some time with Nicky back in Puget Sound. We're old friends."

Randolph threw several more oranges into the water. Each one a little closer to the dinghy.

"One day I dropped my lunch into the water and Nicky ate the whole thing," Randolph said. "After that, she wouldn't leave me alone. I finally figured it out. She has this thing for oranges."

Out in the water, the trail of oranges leading to the dinghy started to disappear, one after the next. Then one flew out of the water toward the inflatable. Jesse reached up and caught it.

"She also likes to play with her food," Randolph added.

Nicky swam up beside the dinghy and opened her mouth, revealing a big grin full of orange peels and pulp. Randolph tossed another orange to her.

Willy swam up to the other side of the dinghy and chattered happily. Meanwhile, Jesse took the transmitter tag and clipped it to Willy's dorsal fin. "There. Now we can find you, no matter where you go."

"And while we've got their attention," Randolph said, "let's check these two out."

He attached an electronic heart monitor to Nicky's head and hooked up the heart monitor to the computer. Jesse watched as his friend's expression became one of concern.

"Something wrong?" he asked.

"I'm not sure," Randolph replied.

"Is she sick?" Jesse asked.

Instead of answering, Randolph directed Jesse to look at the computer monitor. There was definitely something weird going on. Nicky's heartbeat was doubled up. One beat was slow, the other fast.

"What is it?" he asked.

Randolph grinned. "Well, either Nicky has two hearts or . . ." He trailed off, making them guess.

Drew was the one who figured it out. "Or she's going to have a baby."

And with that, as if they knew the examination was over, Willy and Nicky swam away.

19

In the wheelhouse, Sanderson was looking through binoculars for whales and Dineen was listening for them on the hydrophone. Max stuck his head in.

"Can I be the look-out?" he asked.

Sanderson and Dineen shared a glance, then the first mate handed the binoculars to Max.

"You're the captain's kid," Sanderson said ruefully. "You can do whatever you want."

Max pressed the binoculars to his eyes and scanned the horizon. This was part of his campaign *not* to find any more whales. At least if he saw them, he wouldn't have to tell anyone.

For a while, his prayers came true. Max scanned leisurely back and forth. Then he saw something he'd been hoping not to see — a plume of vapor in the distance, followed by the splash of a tail.

"See anything, kid?" Dineen asked behind him.

"Oh, uh, not a thing," Max replied as calmly as he could and started to scan from side to side again. But out of the corner of his eye he saw Dineen suddenly look by at the hydrophone console and start turning dials. "Ahem!" he cleared his throat loudly.

Sanderson spun around, caught his eye, and took the binoculars from Max.

"Starboard, two o'clock, three hundred yards," Dineen said. Max felt his spirits sink. They'd found the whales!

Sanderson fixed the spot with the binoculars. "Kujira!"

"What's kujira?" Max asked.

Sanderson ignored him and yelled at Dineen to sound the horn. A split second later there were sounds of hurried footsteps everywhere. Max's dad stuck his head into the wheelhouse with a big smile on his face. "You ready, Max?"

"Okay," Max replied reluctantly.

"Let's go fishing!" his father said.

Max followed him out to the harpoon cannon, knowing his father was wrong. It wasn't fishing, it was *hunting*.

Blood sport.

Max stepped behind the harpoon cannon, knowing that was what his father expected of him. He reached up and placed his hand on the cold metal of the trigger.

"See 'em, Max?" his father asked behind him.

Max nodded. How could he miss the whales? The *Botany Bay* was headed right for them.

"Sight right down the barrel of the cannon," his father said behind him. "Don't release until I tell you."

"Okay," Max said. It was weird. He could feel the excitement of his father and the rest of the crew. *Two hundred dollars a pound!* they must've been thinking.

His father's lips were right next to his ear. "Remember, Max, aim where the target is going to be, not where it is. If you aim at the target, you're guaranteed to miss."

Guaranteed. The word was music to Max's ear. He aimed directly at the closest whale he saw.

"Ready?" his father hissed into his ear and squeezed his shoulder.

"Ready," Max replied.

"Hold it . . . hold it . . . Now!"

Max squeezed the trigger and felt the recoil as the harpoon fired. *Boom!* The harpoon slashed into the water a dozen feet behind the whale.

"No!" his father cried and quickly but gently nudged Max from behind the cannon. "Hand me another harpoon!"

Sanderson started for a harpoon, but Max pressed himself between them. "I got it!"

"Hurry!" his father yelled.

Max picked up the harpoon, but pretended to fumble with it and got tangled in the line.

"Drop it!" John Wesley barked impatiently.

Max dropped it.

"Step aside," his father ordered.

Max did as he was told. Sanderson quickly lifted a third harpoon and loaded the cannon. Max's father swiveled the big gun around and trained it at the pod of whales, now swimming directly across the bow.

Max was determined to stop him before he killed another whale. Looking around, he saw a ship appear in the distance.

"Dad, look!" He quickly pointed. "A ship!"

Max had hoped only to distract his father long enough for him to miss. He hadn't expected what came next. Both his father and Sanderson narrowed their eyes and squinted at the approaching vessel.

John Wesley looked back at the whales and got behind the cannon. He started to aim, but Sanderson put his hand on his shoulder.

"Don't, Captain," he said gravely. "They'll see us."

Max's father kept his bead on the whales. Max held his breath. Nothing happened. John Wesley had decided not to fire. Muttering to himself, he looked back into the wheelhouse at Dineen and drew his finger across his throat.

Dineen got the message and turned the *Botany Bay* away from the pod of whales. Meanwhile,

Sanderson and Max's father quickly dismantled the harpoon cannon and brought it below decks.

In the meantime, Max stayed on deck, watching the approaching boat and wondering if there was any way they could save him.

20

Jesse and Randolph stood together at the bow of the *Noah*. Randolph studied the ship in the distance through his binoculars. The boat was almost exactly where Willy's pod had been headed. It had appeared to Jesse that the boat had been chasing something, then suddenly changed course and slowed down when the *Noah* came into sight. It could have been nothing, but it seemed suspicious.

"Whalers?" Jesse asked.

"No harpoon," Randolph replied without taking his eyes from the glasses.

Suddenly the boat ahead of them seemed to shudder and the men on board all grabbed for the rail as if the boat had hit something . . . or something had hit the boat. Then a familiar-looking curled dorsal fin broke the surface.

"It's Willy!" Jesse gasped.

Willy's big tail rose in the air and slammed down on the water, sending a spray that drenched the men on the other boat. Jesse narrowed his eyes and felt himself fill with anger.

"It's them, Randolph," he muttered. "Willy wouldn't do that if it wasn't them."

Randolph lowered the binoculars and nodded. "Let's talk to Captain Drake."

Except for the incident with the soot-covered binoculars, Jesse had not had much to do with the captain of the *Noah*. It was clear that the man ran a tight ship and did it by the book, but Jesse had been unable to get a true read on him.

Now that was about to change.

"You have to call this in," Jesse insisted. He was speaking to Captain Drake. They were standing on the deck. Randolph, Drew, First Mate Stevens, and a few other members of the crew were there.

"There's nothing to call in," the captain replied.

"But you saw it yourself," Jesse said. "Willy went after that ship. He would only do that to protect himself. Which means they attacked him."

"You know that for a fact?" First Mate Stevens asked.

"Of course," Jesse replied. "It's obvious if you'd open your eyes."

Stevens and Captain Drake stiffened. They weren't used to being addressed that way by a seventeen-year-old.

"The *Botany Bay* checks out," Captain Drake replied. "It's a registered salmon boat. Its captain,

71

John Wesley, is licensed and his record is spot-less."

Jesse couldn't believe how thick these guys were. "You're right. If he really were a whaler he would have a neon sign flashing, 'Arrest me, I kill whales.'"

Captain Drake was unflappable. "You expect me to tell the coastal marine patrol that a *whale* told us there are whalers here? You'd be able to hear their laughter without a radio." He turned to the first mate. "Stevens, set a course for port."

"Yes, sir," Stevens replied.

"I don't believe it," Jesse sputtered. "They're killing whales and you're going to let them go."

"We are due in port and port is where we are going," Captain Drake replied firmly, and turned away.

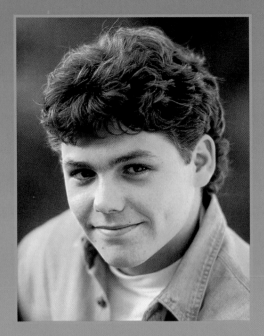

Jesse, now seventeen, sets sail on a mission that could reunite him with his old friend Willy.

Jesse is part of the crew of the *Noah*, helping Drew and his friend Randolph track whales almost anywhere on the planet.

Meanwhile,
another boat isn't
too far away —
the *Botany Bay.*
Max is sailing with
his father, Captain
Wesley, for the
first time!

A new friend! Willy thinks, having spotted Max.

Back at the *Noah*, Jesse signals for Willy by playing his song over an underwater microphone.

Wesley teaches Max how to harpoon whales.

To get Wesley to turn the boat around, Max falls overboard.

Max tries to tell
Wesley he doesn't
want to hurt whales.

Old friends meet again.

"Something is wrong with Willy," Jesse says as he joins Willy in the water. There he discovers Willy's tail has a spear lodged in it!

"Let's give Willy and Nicky a treat," suggests Randolph.
So Jesse tosses them some oranges.

Jesse searches for evidence of illegal whaling on the
Botany Bay.

While Jesse is searching the boat, Max catches him in the act. To win Max's support, Jesse befriends him and takes him out to meet Willy.

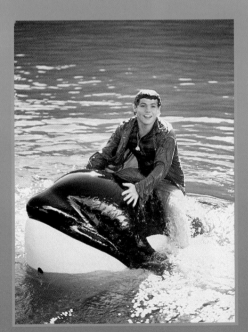

Jesse shows Max how to play Willy's favorite game.

Wesley fears for his life as Willy swims toward him. Willy, although angry at Wesley for injuring him, saves Wesley from certain death.

Wesley holds Max and says, "I know you're right, son. It is wrong to kill whales."
"Maybe whales," Randolph suggests, "are more human than we are."

21

Max stood in the bow of the *Botany Bay*. Thanks to a great deal of luck, he'd managed to stop them from killing any whales today. But he wondered what would happen tomorrow.

He heard footsteps and turned to see his father approaching. An odd, unexpected feeling of appreciation welled up inside him as he remembered how badly his father had wanted that whale, and how badly he, Max, had intentionally messed things up. Any other father would have lost his temper, or worse.

But not his father. His father was a good man. A good man who was doing something bad. It still didn't make sense to Max.

"What's kujira?" Max asked.

His father raised an eyebrow. "Where'd you pick that up?"

"Sanderson," Max said. "That's what he called them."

"Kujira is sushi made from killer whales," his father said. "We harvest the meat and sell it to the Japanese. To eat."

Max nodded. His father chuckled, as if at some private joke. "Know what your grandfather would say about that?"

Max shook his head.

"He would say, 'Is that God's work, son? Finding sushi for the Japanese?' "

Max frowned. "I don't get it."

"God's work." John Wesley gazed wistfully out at the ocean. "That's what Dad said whaling was. Because for hundreds of years, the whales they killed made oil that filled the lamps that lit the world. Whales made *light*, Max. It was work that meant something then."

Max looked up at his father. "What does it mean now?"

"It means you have a right to be what you are," his father replied. "You have a right to make a living."

22

Jesse stood at the gunwale and stared at the *Botany Bay* through the binoculars.

Whale killers, he thought. And what really irked him was that it looked like they'd brought some kid with them. Like they were training the next generation in the fine art of murdering large, endangered mammals.

Drew came up beside him and leaned against the gunwale.

"Drake's a jerk," Jesse muttered without taking his eyes off the other boat.

"You just noticed?" Drew replied.

"I thought maybe you were going to tell me he was just doing his job," Jesse said, studying her warily.

"He is just doing his job," she said.

"And the whalers are doing their jobs." Jesse's words were filled with disgust. "And we're going to follow orders and do nothing to stop them."

"We're all trying to do the right thing," Drew

said. "But I'm just a marine biologist. I don't have super powers. And neither do you."

"Right." Jesse screwed his mouth up contemptuously. "We just do research. Whale-killing isn't our problem . . . But it's *my* problem."

Drew sighed and nodded as if to show that it was her problem, too. "If you keep this up, you're going to get me fired."

Jesse smiled at her and jerked his head toward the hatch that led below deck. They went down to The Pit and Jesse plugged his laptop into the hydrophone. Randolph came in.

"What's up?" the older man asked.

"We're activating the Willy Pager again," Jesse said. "If we can't follow the whales, maybe we can get the whales to follow us. That way we can keep an eye on them."

The skin around Randolph's eyes wrinkled as he peered down at the laptop's screen.

"What's wrong?" Jesse asked him.

"We can't keep an eye on them all the time," Randolph said. "Maybe tomorrow, maybe a year from now, those killers will find them. And we won't be there to do anything about it."

23

Max and his father were still talking when Sanderson appeared behind them. "Sorry, Captain."

"I'm talking to my kid," John Wesley replied.

Sanderson nodded as if he understood. "You're going to want to hear this."

"Come on," Wesley said to his son. Max followed him to the wheelhouse. It pained him that his father was so eager to teach him about whaling. Inside the wheelhouse, Kron was fiddling with the hydrophone and the old reel-to-reel tape recorder. The Willy Pager sound was coming out of a speaker.

"The sound that doesn't quite sound like a whale," Sanderson said.

Kron pointed through the window at the *Noah*. "It's coming from that boat."

"Do we know what it is yet?" Wesley said.

"No, but I can tell you this," Kron said. "Every time we find whales, that boat isn't far behind."

"They play that sound and the whales come," Sanderson said. "Now you have it on tape, right?"

"That's right," Kron replied.

"So we could broadcast it ourselves," Max's father said.

"Not quite," Kron said. "But after a quick stop in port for some key parts, we sure could."

Captain Wesley nodded and smiled as he gazed out at the *Noah* again. "If they can do it, so can we."

24

They'd docked at an old wooden pier of a small fishing village. Jesse had always been sort of mystified by places like this. On one hand, he loved the idea of a place that had such a direct relationship with the sea. On the other hand, it was so isolated from the rest of the world.

Even now, as he walked along the rickety wooden dock, past the slips where the fishermen sat in their boats, mending nets and fixing electronics, he could feel their eyes on him. He was a stranger here, and he'd just come off a big metal ship twice the size of their largest fishing vessel. No wonder they regarded him with suspicion.

Jesse followed the dock to the shore, then turned to look out at the bay. But his eyes focused on someone on the dock parallel to the one he'd just walked down. A kid was standing there, leaning against the wooden rail. A familiar-looking kid. Jesse couldn't be certain, but he looked an awful lot like the kid he'd seen standing on the deck of the *Botany Bay*.

Something small dropped out of the kid's hands and down into the shallow surf under the pier. The kid made no motion to try and catch it. Nor did he race down to the end of the pier and out onto the beach. He just walked away.

Jesse was curious. Trying not to attract too much attention, he left the pier he was standing on and strolled down the beach. He was wearing his rubber boating boots, so it was no trouble to step into the water and retrieve what the kid had dropped.

Jesse picked the wet thing up in his hand. It was some kind of necklace with a carving. He blinked as he realized what it was — a carving of a harpoon tip. Jesse studied it closer, its ivory color and the tiny faint brown fissures. Whale tooth. Jesse squeezed the carving with anger until his knuckles turned white. He stared up at the pier, but the kid was gone.

That didn't mean he couldn't find him. Jesse started back up the beach. He was angry, of course, but also puzzled. Why had the kid dropped it?

Jesse climbed up to the pier. There he was! Down at the other end. Jesse started to jog. He was just about to call out when he saw something that made him stop. The kid went up a short wooden gangplank and got on an old fishing boat

with car tires hammered to the bow. Her name
was *Botany Bay.*

So that *was* the kid, Jesse thought, turning
around. He was going to find Randolph and tell
him.

He was walking down the small main street,
just passing a cafe, when he heard someone knock
on glass. Turning around, he saw Randolph inside
the cafe on a pay phone. Randolph gestured for
him to come inside, then put his hand over the re-
ceiver and whispered for Jesse to get them a couple of cups of coffee.

Jesse slid into a booth and ordered two coffees
from an attractive older woman with red hair.
They had a short friendly conversation in which
she noted that he was a stranger in town. Jesse
said only that he was part of the crew on a marine
biology vessel, but he appreciated the fact that
she was friendly.

A moment later Randolph slid into the booth.

"Any luck?" Jesse asked.

Randolph shook his head. "Nope. The coastal
marine patrol isn't interested in *suspected*
whalers. They told me to call back when I had
proof."

"And what do they call proof?" Jesse asked as
the lady returned and filled their cups with coffee.

"Short of catching them red-handed, I have no
idea," Randolph said.

"Anything else I can get you?" the woman asked.

"No, thanks," Randolph said. She left a check on the table.

Jesse put his elbows on the table and leaned forward. "If we could get on board the *Botany Bay* we'd get all the proof we needed.

"On board the *Botany Bay?*" Randolph gave him a dubious look. "A boat filled with whalers? Are you crazy?"

Jesse shrugged. "Yeah, I guess that won't work."

They finished their coffees and left the cafe. Out on the street, the locals gave them more funny looks.

"I'd like to poke around," Randolph said. "Talk to a few people. Maybe I can turn up some hard evidence."

Jesse doubted it. "Maybe you haven't noticed that we stick out like sore thumbs around here. Asking them questions is about as dangerous as sneaking onto whaling boats."

"And that's why you're going back to the *Noah*," Randolph said.

Jesse stopped. "I am?"

"I know you, Jess," Randolph said. "I already told Drew to find something to keep you busy."

"But —"

Randolph shook his head. "No arguments. I

promised Glen and Annie you'd be safe. Now go on, back to the ship. Drew's expecting you."

Jesse nodded and left Randolph there on the corner. He headed back toward the *Noah*.

And right past it.

To the *Botany Bay*.

25

Max was sitting on a tackle box, undoing a strand of nylon rope. He was trying to get up the nerve to tell his father a lie when a guy in black rubber boots stepped onto the *Botany Bay*. The guy had curly blond hair and appeared to be just a few years older than Max.

"You work on this boat?" the guy asked.

Max nodded.

"What's your name?" the guy asked.

"Max. What's yours?"

"My name?" The guy seemed to hesitate. "Randolph."

That hesitation made Max wary. "What do you want?"

"I'm looking for work," the guy said.

"Doing what?" Max asked.

"I've worked a lot of different boats," the guy replied. "Herring, mackerel, salmon . . ." He paused and lowered his voice. "Orca."

"What's orca?" Max asked.

"You know," the guy said in a low voice. "Whale."

A red light went on in Max's head. Why was this stranger talking to him about whales? Did *everyone* know what his father did?

"I'd like to work a whaling boat," the guy went on. "I don't like whales. They stink."

"Well, I kind of like them," Max replied guardedly. He was relieved to see his father come around the corner and clap a hand on the guy's shoulder. The guy spun around and looked surprised.

"Who's your friend, Max?" John Wesley asked.

"His name is Randolph," Max said.

"Hello." The guy offered his hand. Max's father just stared at it.

"He's looking for work," Max said.

John Wesley shook his head. "Sorry, we're all crewed up. Max, why don't you show your friend out?"

Max got up. "He's not really my friend. I'm going to see Mom, okay?"

"Sure," his father said.

Max left the boat and started down the pier. He wasn't really going to see his mom. He waited until he was out of earshot and then looked back at the guy, who was walking behind him. "Can I ask you a question?"

"Sure," the guy said.

"Why do you want to be a whaler?"

The guy looked surprised. "I ... never really thought about it."

"Why not?" Max asked as they walked.

"Hey, everyone has to make a living, right?" the guy said.

It sounded familiar to Max. It was the same thing his father had said.

"You got a problem with that?" the guy asked.

"Yeah, I do," Max said. "What if someone hunted you? Would you like it?"

"No, I guess not," the guy admitted.

"Then don't do it," Max said.

"Okay," the guy said. "You convinced me. Whaling is wrong."

Max didn't know whether to believe him or not. The guy had agreed too easily. Something wasn't right. Something that went beyond this dork agreeing whaling was wrong. They were passing the library now.

"See you," Max said, and suddenly turned and started up the library steps.

"Hey, Max," the guy called behind him.

Max felt a shiver. He just wanted to get away from the guy. "I gotta go," he called back without stopping.

"Why does your dad like it?" the guy asked.

That made Max stop. He turned around. "My dad is a salmon boat captain."

"Oh?" The guy looked like he didn't believe him.

"Well, he is," Max said, then turned and went into the library.

26

Jesse watched the kid go into the library. Pretending to be a whaler had been stupid, but he wasn't about to give up on his quest. Besides, he was intrigued. First the kid throws away the carved whale tooth, next he says he likes whales. But he goes out on a whaling boat. Something strange was going on.

Jesse climbed the steps and went into the library. He expected the inside to be dark and musty. But it was well lit, with shelves of videotapes as well as books, and brand-new computer terminals with on-line catalogues and Internet browsers.

Cool place, Jesse thought as he looked around for the kid. He found him sitting at a table behind a stack of whaling books. The old black-and-white photos showed the great beasts being skinned and stripped, and the huge caldrons for melting the blubber down into oil for lamps.

Jesse sat down across from the kid, who quickly shut the book.

"I lied to you," Jesse said. "I'm not a whaler and I'm not looking for work."

The kid slid a book onto his lap and opened it so Jesse couldn't see. "So what?" he pretended not to care.

"Actually, I'm sort of the opposite," Jesse said.

The kid looked up. "You're a whale?"

"I'm trying to protect them," Jesse said. He expected the kid to look back down at the book, but he didn't. Jesse decided to gamble. "What your dad's doing is wrong. I think you know that."

"My dad's a salmon boat captain," the kid said automatically.

"Right." Jesse nodded like he didn't believe it for a second.

"Why do you care anyway?" the kid asked.

"If a friend of yours was in trouble, you'd help him, wouldn't you?" Jesse said.

"Sure," the kid said. "I mean, if I could."

Jesse leaned forward. "Your dad is hurting my friends."

Max leaned back in his chair. "I don't know what you're talking about."

"Yeah, you do," Jesse said, getting up. "Come on, I'll show you."

The kid looked up at him. "How?"

"You want to meet them, don't you?" Jesse said. "I'll introduce you. I think they'll like you."

27

The blond guy's name was Jesse, not Randolph, and he had this thing called a transmitter that was hooked to a computer and could actually follow whales electronically and pinpoint them on maps. The next thing Max knew, he and Jesse were riding in the dinghy along the coast just north of the village. Suddenly Jesse cut the engine and the dinghy glided along silently.

"Listen," Jesse said.

Max listened and heard what sounded like strange birdcalls.

"Whale songs," Jesse said, picking up his binoculars. "That's quite a sound, isn't it?"

Max nodded silently.

"Did you know that when he sings you can feel the beat of his song in time with the waves?" Jesse asked as he scanned the horizon.

Max shook his head. He'd never heard of such a thing. But as he listened and watched the waves, he saw that it was true. The song and the waves were in time.

"Why do they do that?" he asked.

"*I* think it's because they're great musicians," Jesse answered. "But a friend of mine has a different theory. He says it's because the whole earth is breathing. It's the song of the earth breathing."

Jesse pointed, then handed Max the binoculars. "There they are."

Max took the binoculars and pressed them to his eyes. The first whale he saw was the one with the curled dorsal fin. "Oh, *him!*"

Jesse scowled. "You know him?"

"We've met," Max said, reaching over the side of the dinghy. He wet his fingers and then rubbed them along the side of the inflatable, making a squeaking sound.

"What's that supposed to do?" Jesse asked.

"Wait," Max said, and did it again.

This time Willy answered with a squeak of his own. Max turned to Jesse and grinned triumphantly. "Want to try it?"

"That's okay," Jesse replied.

"Come on, it's easy," Max said, making more squeaking noises. "Don't be afraid."

Jesse rolled his eyes. "I'm not afraid."

Willy surfaced next to the dinghy. Suddenly the inflatable lurched forward. Max grabbed for an oarlock, remembering how the whale had rammed the *Botany Bay*. He was certain they were going to get capsized.

Jesse looked amused. "Don't be afraid," he said in a teasing voice.

"I'm not afraid," Max replied, nervously clinging to the oarlock.

The whale gave them a ride in a big circle around the bay, but didn't try to capsize them, much to Max's relief. Finally they wound up in a small cove near the shore. The whale disappeared.

Max looked over the side. "Where'd he go?"

As if in answer, the dinghy started to rock. No doubt the whale was under them, doing the rocking. Max grabbed for the oarlock again.

"He likes to play games," Jesse said.

"What games does he know?" Max asked.

"Fetch," Jesse answered. "Fetch is his favorite."

"What does he fetch?" Max asked.

Instead of answering, Jesse stood up and said, "Just do everything I do."

Then jumped!

Max watched in disbelief as Jesse hit the water. A second later his head came up and he treaded water near the dinghy.

"Isn't it freezing?" Max asked, remembering his own recent dip in the ocean.

"It's not so bad here in the shallows," Jesse said. "The sun warms the water. Trust me."

Max took a deep breath and jumped. He felt the

chill as he went under, then opened his eyes. To his astonishment, a huge black figure was right in front of him! The next thing he knew, the whale pressed his snout under Max's stomach and pushed him up to the surface.

"Cool!" Max gasped, facing Jesse. "He fetched *me*. Can we do it again?"

"As much as you like," Jesse answered.

Later they got cold and climbed back into the dinghy to dry off. Max noticed that Jesse was watching him closely.

"What is it?" Max asked.

"I've never seen him take to anyone like that before," Jesse replied.

"I thought maybe he was like that with everyone," Max said.

"No, he's only like that with family," Jesse replied mysteriously.

Family? What was Jesse talking about? "I'm not his family," Max said.

Jesse just smiled. "Tell *him* that."

28

They were headed back to the village in the dinghy. Jesse sat in the back and steered. Max was in the bow.

"Doing stuff with whales is your job?" Max asked.

"Yeah." Jesse nodded.

"You like it?"

"Yeah."

"I didn't know people had jobs like that," Max said.

"Neither did I," Jesse replied with a smile.

Max pointed into an inlet lined with tall spruce. "Turn in there."

"Why?" Jesse asked.

"You'll see."

As they went into the inlet, a small cedar shake house with a green roof came into view, nestled in the trees. Smoke curled out of a chimney and the air smelled like wood smoke. Jesse tied the dinghy up at a small dock while Max hopped out and ran up to the house. Jesse followed him inside and found him standing in the hall, looking at pictures on the wall.

They were pictures of whalers.

"That's my family," Max said.

"Big family," Jesse said. "What's it like?"

"Just like any family," Max said with a shrug. "You know."

"No, I don't," Jesse said. "Not every kid has a family. I didn't always. You're lucky."

They stood side by side, looking at the photographs. Now Jesse understood something he hadn't understood before. Max's people were whalers. They'd *always* been whalers.

"You like your dad?" Jesse asked.

Max nodded. "He's a good dad. A good person."

Jesse let out a sigh and shook his head. It sort of explained why Max could be on a whaling boat and still like whales. The kid was in a tough spot. "Then I can't ask you to help. Even if he's doing something wrong, he's still your dad."

"I thought you wanted my help," Max said.

"I did," Jesse said. "But I can't ask you to do that. I'll stop him myself."

29

Drew found Randolph sitting on a bench outside the fish processing plant.

"I've been looking all over for you," she said, sitting down next to him.

"I've been here all afternoon," Randolph said.

"Just sitting on this bench?" Drew asked.

"Sitting on this bench . . . watching." Randolph nodded toward the fish processing plant. A group of fishermen were waiting in line outside a window. One by one they went up to the window and handed a piece of paper to a man inside. The man then paid them.

"So what's the big deal?" Drew asked.

"Each boat captain brings his boat to the plant and offloads his catch," Randolph explained. "In return he gets a piece of paper. On it is the type of fish he caught and the total weight. The captain takes that piece of paper to the guy in the window. The guy in the window tallies up the price per pound times the number of pounds and hands the captain his money and a receipt for the fish."

"Right," Drew said. "That's how fishermen make their living. So what else is new?"

"Watch," Randolph said. As they watched, each captain in line got paid. Soon only John Wesley was left. He reached into his pocket and slipped something to the man in the window.

"Is it my imagination, or was that money?" Drew whispered.

"It was not your imagination," Randolph whispered back.

A moment later, the man in the window handed John Wesley a receipt. Drew wrinkled her nose. "Could you explain to me what just happened?"

"I'd be delighted," Randolph said. "What you just witnessed was a bribe. He paid the guy in the window for a phony receipt. So he gets a receipt for salmon that never existed, and the guy in the window reports the sale to the fishery bureau. Everything seems perfectly legal. No questions asked."

"Except he never catches any salmon," Drew said.

"Sort of makes you wonder what he's really catching, doesn't it?" Randolph asked.

Drew nodded and looked around. "By the way, where's Jesse?"

Randolph straightened up. "He was supposed to be on the *Noah* with you."

Drew shook her head. "Haven't seen him since this morning."

30

Jesse thought he had it well planned. He knew Randolph would be searching for him, so he left a collar mike and earpiece on his bunk. Now he, Jesse, was standing in the shadows on the deck of the *Botany Bay*. If the coastal marine patrol wanted hard evidence, he'd get it for them.

"Jesse?" He welcomed the sound of Randolph's voice in his earpiece.

"Hey, man, you found it." Jesse congratulated him.

"Where are you?" Randolph asked urgently, obviously not in the mood to play around.

"I'm getting the proof we need," Jesse replied.

"*Where are you?*" Randolph demanded, this time even more urgently.

"If I tell you, you have to promise not to be mad," Jesse said.

But Randolph didn't have to be told anything. He knew Jesse too well. "Do you have any idea what they'll do to you if they catch you?"

Jesse stepped out of the shadows and switched on a penlight, looking around the *Botany Bay*'s deck with the tiny beam. "Do you have any idea what they'll do to Willy if they catch *him*?" he asked back.

"For Pete's sake!" Randolph sputtered into the collar mike.

"Listen," Jesse said. "Wesley's in the bar in town. Do me a favor and make sure he doesn't get back until I'm gone. I don't want this tub leaving port with me aboard."

"Jesse —" Randolph started to say.

But Jesse heard footsteps and the sound of a man whistling. "Someone's coming," he whispered into the collar mike. "Gotta book. Sorry."

He pressed himself into the shadows again. The whistling man was coming closer. Jesse held his breath. The whistling man walked past, carrying a box of some sort, then went into the wheelhouse. Jesse stayed frozen, barely allowing himself to breathe. How long would he have to wait?

31

Max was lying on his side in bed, the covers pulled up under his chin. His mom came to the door and looked surprised.

"Already in bed?"

"Yeah."

She creased her forehead. "Something wrong?"

Max nodded. "What do you do if someone is trying to make you do something you don't want to do?"

"Who?" his mom asked.

"Just someone," Max said.

"You should never let other people tell you what to do," his mom said. "You have to stick up for yourself. Do what you think is right."

"What if it hurts?" Max asked.

"That's hard," his mom admitted. "But you still should do it."

"Is that what *you* do, Mom?" Max asked.

Mary Wesley came into the room and sat down

on the edge of the bed. She brushed her son's hair across his forehead. "I try my best."

Max looked into his mom's eyes. "What happens if they catch him?"

Mrs. Wesley blinked as if she now understood what her son had been getting at. "Your father? He would never get caught."

"Suppose he did," Max said. "Would he have to go away? Like to jail?"

"Oh, no," his mom said. "Is that what you're worried about?"

Max nodded.

"No," she said. "He would never have to go to jail."

"Then what would happen?" Max asked.

"Well, they might take his boat away and make him pay a fine," she supposed.

"You promise that's all?" Max asked.

"Yes," his mom said. "Your father loves you very much. You know that, don't you?"

Max nodded.

"He does what he does for you and me," Mrs. Wesley said. "To make us happy and put a roof over our heads and bug warriors on TV."

"But don't you ever wish he would stop?" Max asked. "Don't you wish he would do something else?"

His mother blinked and didn't answer. For a second Max thought he saw the answer in her eyes. Then she leaned over and kissed him on the forehead. "I love you, Max."

"You could tell him," Max said as his mother started to get up. "He would listen to you."

But his mother shook her head. "I love him and I believe in him. For better or for worse."

She turned off the light and closed the door. Max waited, then quietly slipped out of bed. He was fully clothed. He went to his bedroom window, slid it open, and quietly climbed out.

32

There were two men in the wheelhouse, but they were busy working on something. Jesse took a chance and started to poke around again with his pencil-thin flashlight. He looked over the places in the bow where a harpoon cannon might have been mounted, but there was no sign of anything suspicious.

Suddenly the wheelhouse door opened. Jesse had no place to hide. A man came out and started down the deck in the opposite direction, then went across the gangplank to the dock.

Jesse breathed a sigh of relief and kept searching. He found a hatch in the deck and slowly pulled it open. Shining his light inside, he saw it glint off something metal. It was time to get back on the mike.

"Hey, Randolph, where are you?" he whispered.

"In the bar, just like you ordered," Randolph whispered back sourly.

"Good," Jesse said, "because I think I found something."

"Listen, you better get out of there now," Randolph warned him. "Your friends are leaving."

"You have to buy me some time," Jesse said.

"What do you expect me to do?" came the reply.

"How do I know?" Jesse said. "Ask them to dance."

"Sorry, they're not my type," Randolph said.

"Come on, man, do something," Jesse said. "I'm going below deck. Wish me luck."

"Good luck," Randolph muttered with a sigh.

Holding the penlight in his mouth, Jesse lowered himself through the hatch. Through the earpiece he could hear the noise of the bar, then Randolph's voice hailing John Wesley.

It was pitch-black in the hold. Jesse fanned the flashlight around, looking for a light switch. In his ear he heard Randolph trying to talk Wesley into having a drink.

Jesse found a switch and flicked it on. With a start he found himself crouched next to the harpoon cannon. Talk about hard evidence! Jesse spoke into his collar mike. "Hey, Randolph, I hit the jackpot! Randolph?"

All he got back was static. Jesse reached up to the earpiece and raised the volume. Now he could hear crashing sounds and grunts and shouts. It sounded just like . . . a bar brawl!

"Hey, come on," he said. "No fooling around. This is serious. Randolph?"

But all he heard was more bar brawl. Jesse had a feeling the collar mike was no longer on Randolph's collar. Besides, there was another room down there. He squeezed himself through a second hatch and flicked on a light.

Geez! It was a whale torture chamber! Jesse stared in awe at the flensing knives, picks, and saws. He ran his finger over the exploding harpoon heads and the spears. Okay, he'd seen enough. It was definitely time to get going. He decided to take a spear for evidence to show the coastal marine patrol. And he'd leave these guys a little present as well — a transmitter tag hidden in the gear so that he'd be able to track them on the computer.

He grabbed the spear and pushed open the hatch. He managed to get the spear through and was just about to follow when he heard footsteps. A lot of them.

33

Jesse ducked back down into the hold, angry at himself for leaving the spear on deck. He could hear footsteps all over the deck above him. There were at least three and possibly four men up there, and they were moving fast. Jesse felt a sick sensation rise in his stomach. Men on boats didn't move at that pace . . . unless they were in a hurry to leave.

The big diesel engine roared to life. Jesse knew he had to do something fast. Once they were out to sea, they might stay there for weeks! Sooner or later they'd find him and he'd become shark bait.

The boat lurched. Darn it! They were underway. Jesse quickly cast about for a way out. He jammed his hand into his pocket and came up with that carved whale tooth necklace. Suddenly he had an idea.

He went through a door and into the engine compartment. The tart scent of fuel hit his nose. The big eight-cylinder diesel sat in the middle of the compartment, chugging away. Jesse opened the flap that provided access to the timing gears. He shoved an old rag into the engine. As he did so, the whale tooth necklace caught on a lever and was left behind.

The engine instantly sputtered and made loud, screeching, grinding sounds. Acrid smoke started to fill the engine compartment. Jesse could hear shouts coming from above as the men sensed something was wrong. He went back through the door and into the forward hold. Now was the time to escape.

Once again, Jesse pushed open the deck hatch and climbed out. His plan was to grab the spear and get off the boat fast. But on the deck he discovered the spear was gone!

What the . . . ?

Someone tapped him on the shoulder. Jesse spun around and raised his fists. But it was Max, crouching in the dark behind him, holding up the spear.

"You dropped this," Max said.

Jesse stared at him for a second, then crouched down and took the spear back. "What are you doing here?"

"Getting into trouble," Max replied.

Jesse smirked. "Me, too."

"So what are we gonna do?" Max asked.

Jesse peered over the gunwale. The boat was only a few dozen yards from the pier. "We're going to swim back."

Max shook his head. "You go. I'll stay here and do what I can to help."

The kid had guts, but Jesse still didn't like the idea. "I told you I didn't want you to get into trouble.

Max responded with a shrug. "Hey, I'm just a kid, right?"

Jesse had to smile. Then, clenching the spear tightly, he vaulted over the gunwale and into the dark waters below.

By the time Jesse reached the bar in town, he was shivering. His clothes were soaked and he was carrying two spears. The whole one he'd just taken from the *Botany Bay*, and the broken one he'd pulled out of Willy's tail a few days before.

Inside the bar, First Mate Stevens and Captain Drake sat at a table covered with empty bottles. Stevens's hair was ruffled, and the captain's tie hung loosely around his collar. It appeared that they'd both had plenty to drink.

Jesse nodded at Randolph and Drew, then slammed both spears on the table in front of Captain Drake and Stevens. "There's your proof."

Both men looked up at him as if they didn't know what the heck he was talking about.

Jesse pointed at the broken spear. "I pulled this one out of an orca's tail two days ago." Then he pointed at the whole spear. "And I just took this one off the *Botany Bay*."

"I see," Captain Drake rubbed his chin.

"We were right," said Randolph.

"So it would seem," Drake replied.

"We have to stop them," Jesse said.

"Yes." Drake nodded. "I'll call this into the coastal marine patrol first thing in the morning."

Jesse couldn't believe his ears. He turned to Randolph, begging him with his eyes to say something.

"In the morning it'll be too late," Randolph said.

"They're on their way out right now," Jesse said. "They're going for whales. We can catch them red-handed."

"Listen," Captain Drake replied. "My job isn't law enforcement. That's the coastal marine patrol's job. I'm not about to risk a two-million-dollar ship to do their job. My job is to call it in for you. That's it."

"And by the way," Stevens added. "The coastal marine patrol's going to want to review the evidence before they make a ruling."

"Make a ruling?" Jesse replied in disbelief. "But that'll take days. We can act now."

Captain Drake shook his head. "Listen, kid, you did good. I'm impressed. But we still have to follow procedure. Now why don't you let me buy you a soda?"

Jesse clenched and unclenched his fists. He really wanted to let Drake have it, but he had to think about Willy and the other whales. He forced himself to calm down. "Thanks for the offer, sir, but I should probably get some sleep. Good night, sir, and thanks for all you've done."

"It was nothing," Captain Drake replied.

Jesse turned away. Drake certainly was right about *that*. He'd done nothing and could be expected to do nothing in the future, too. Jesse headed out of the bar and down the street. He heard footsteps behind him and turned to see Randolph.

"Can I ask you a hypothetical question?" Jesse asked the older man.

Randolph rolled his eyes. "I'm afraid of your hypothetical questions, Jesse. They have a habit of not being so hypothetical."

"So I guess you don't want to hear the question," Jesse said.

"Ten years in jail," Randolph said.

Jesse winced. "Just for borrowing a boat that doesn't belong to you?"

"It's called *piracy*," Randolph said. "Ten years in the slammer. Do not pass Go. Do not collect two hundred dollars."

Jesse sighed. "Sounds like a pretty bad idea."

Randolph nodded. "Right. So let's do it."

A little while later, Jesse undid the mooring lines to the *Noah*, while Randolph searched through First Mate Stevens's cabin for the key to start the engines. He found a small metal lockbox and started to pry it open.

"Looking for something?" a voice behind him asked.

Randolph turned around and found Drew in the doorway. "I'm looking for the spare start key," he said.

"You're stealing the boat," Drew said. "And going after the whalers."

"Looks like it," Randolph said.

"They'll notice the *Noah*'s gone," Drew said. "You'll go to jail."

"I can live with that," Randolph replied.

"Why?" Drew asked.

"It's the right thing to do."

"You work for me, Randolph," Drew said. "You understand that, don't you?"

Randolph kept trying to pry open the box. "Well, looks like you're going to have to fire me."

Drew looked at him for a long time, then sighed and reached into her pocket. She took out the start key and held it up for him to see. "Is this what you're looking for?"

Randolph looked surprised, then took the key.

"What if I order you to ready the *Noah* for immediate departure?" Drew asked.

"You'll lose your job," Randolph replied.

"Hey, they told me to keep an eye on you," Drew said with a shrug. "I'm just doing my job."

34

Max lay in the berth in his father's cabin in the dark, listening to the activity. The crew had managed to fix the problem with the diesel and now the *Botany Bay* was chugging out to sea. The heavy clanking sounds meant that they were mounting the harpoon cannon on the bow. He'd heard snippets of talk about the hydrophone and some new whale call. It sounded like they weren't going to have to chase the whales this time. Instead, they would get the whales to come to them.

Botany Bay, Max thought. Funny that when he'd finally looked it up in the library, it turned out to be a place where criminals were sent.

The door opened and Max's dad came in and flicked on the light. Max squinted up at him in the sudden brightness. "Hi, Dad."

John Wesley looked surprised. "What are you doing here, Max?"

"I was looking for you," Max replied innocently. "Guess I fell asleep. What's going on?"

"Go back to sleep," his father said. "I'll tell you in the morning."

The morning came too quickly. When Max woke up, his father's berth was already empty. Max pulled on his clothes and went above decks. A fog hung over the surface of the ocean. He couldn't see more than twenty or thirty yards.

He found his father working on the harpoon cannon.

"Sleep well?" his father asked.

Max nodded. "I have a question, Dad."

"Take this," his father said, handing him a small can of oil. "Squeeze some into the gears, okay?"

Max did as he was told. "Why is it wrong to hurt other people?"

"It just is," his father replied. "That's the rule."

"But don't you ever want to just do what you want no matter who it hurts?" Max asked.

"Maybe," John Wesley replied. "But you don't."

"Why not?"

"Because people have rights," his father replied, still working on the harpoon.

"Where do they get them?" Max asked.

"You're born with them, Max. Everybody has them." His father took a lethal-looking harpoon and loaded it into the cannon.

114

"What if whales are like people?" Max asked.

"They're not."

"But what if they are?" Max persisted.

John Wesley stopped what he was doing and looked at his son. "A whale is an animal, Max. Animals were put here by God for us to hunt. You don't get upset when you eat a cheeseburger, do you?"

"Why not?" Max asked.

His father went back to work. "Whales don't feel. They aren't people. They're just fish."

"You're wrong," Max said.

"You know better than me?" his father asked. "You're ten years old."

"You're still wrong, Dad," Max said.

"Right," his father grunted, his face turning red. "I've been wrong all my life. And my dad was wrong. And *his* dad. We're all wrong, and you're right."

"You're hurting people, Dad," Max said.

"Who am I hurting?" his father asked. "I'm not hurting anyone."

"You're hurting me," Max said.

John Wesley locked eyes with his son and gave him an astonished look. Just then Sanderson appeared on the bow.

"Not now!" Wesley snapped at him.

"Sorry, Captain," Sanderson said. "But I finally found that problem with the diesel last night, and I thought you'd like to know." He handed Wesley the whale tooth necklace that he had found in the engine compartment.

John Wesley stared down at it with an incredulous look on his face. Then he turned to his son and spoke very firmly. "Come with me, Max."

35

Jesse was on the bridge of the *Noah* with Randolph and Drew. The fog was thickening, and they were traveling mostly by radar. Jesse was watching two blips on the computer screen. One was Willy's pod, the other was the *Botany Bay*. At the moment, they were both traveling in the same direction. Jesse felt somewhat reassured by the fact that nearly half a dozen miles separated the whales from the whale hunters.

In the meantime, they were sharing a chuckle about Captain Drake and First Mate Stevens.

"I can just see them stumbling back to the dock last night," Randolph said. "And the two of them wandering around trying to figure out where they put their boat."

Jesse smiled, then looked down at the computer screen and froze. He couldn't believe what he was seeing!

"Look at this!" he pointed at the screen. "Willy's

pod just turned completely around! They're heading right for the *Botany Bay*."

Drew looked at the screen and scowled. "Why would they do that?"

The answer hit Jesse like a slap. He dashed out of the bridge and down to The Pit. By the time Randolph arrived, Jesse was getting a reading off the hydrophone.

"It's the Willy Pager," Jesse groaned. "The *Botany Bay*'s playing it. They must've taped it."

"Willy won't know the difference," Randolph said. "He'll lead the pod straight to them."

"Thinking it's me," Jesse added.

Randolph nodded grimly. "They're swimming right into a trap."

Jesse jumped up and headed back to the bridge. Drew was at the helm, her eyes jumping back and forth from the radar screen to the fog-covered waters.

"It's getting bad out there," she said.

"Worse than you think," Jesse said, showing her the computer screen. On the screen, the gap between the pod and the whalers was quickly narrowing. "We better hurry."

Drew bit her lip nervously. "I hate to crank her up in this soup."

"If you don't, there's no reason for us to even be here," Jesse said.

Drew nodded and pushed the throttle forward. "Full steam ahead."

The *Noah*'s bow rose as the ship surged forward.

"Something just occurred to me," Drew said.

"What?" Randolph asked.

"Even if we find them, what are we going to do?"

36

John Wesley had locked his son in his cabin behind the wheelhouse. Max tried the door, but it wouldn't give. He pressed his ear against the door, and heard his father asking Kron where the whales were. Kron answered that they were around three miles away, and closing.

"It's working like a charm, sir," Kron added.

Max waited, praying the whales would change course or just disappear. But a few minutes later he heard Sanderson yell, "There they are! Ten o'clock!"

The *Botany Bay* veered portside. Max knew he had to get out of the cabin. He had to stop them. He spied his dad's knife, the one with the whale-tooth handle, that for so many generations had aided whalers. Well, now it was going to aid the whales. Max grabbed it and jammed it into the door lock.

The door sprang, and Max rushed out. He could see his father on the bow, aiming the harpoon cannon. The other men were busy with ropes and buoys. Through a break in the fog Max saw the whales cavorting on the surface, unaware of the danger that was bearing down on them.

John Wesley aimed down the barrel of the cannon and closed his finger around the trigger. Max knew of only one way to stop him. He put his hands on the pipe rail and shouted, "Dad!"

His father turned.

Max vaulted over the side.

37

The *Noah* was at full throttle. On the bridge, Randolph pointed at the computer screen. The two blips had joined into one.

"We're too late," he said with a grimace.

"We just need a few minutes to catch up," Drew said.

"We don't have it," said Jesse. His head was filled with visions of harpoons and spears and terrified, bleeding whales. The sea frothing red with blood — a scene from the distant past.

Then something on the computer caught his attention. The blip for the *Botany Bay* had suddenly turned around.

"Randolph, look at this." He pointed to the computer screen. "The *Botany Bay* is turning around. They're doing a big circle."

"Why?" Randolph scowled.

Jesse suddenly knew why. It must've been Max. He must've done something.

38

The water out here was a lot colder than in that sunny cove the day before. Max treaded water as the *Botany Bay* came around and his father climbed down a ladder and offered his hand.

"Come on, Max," his father said.

Max treaded water, making no attempt to take his father's hand. "Say you're wrong."

"You'll freeze to death if you don't come out of that water," his father said.

Max knew he was right. His teeth were chattering and his arms and legs were numb. He felt like if he spent another second in that water his limbs would stiffen, and he'd sink. He reached up and let his father take his hand.

John Wesley yanked his son back onto the *Botany Bay*.

"Go!" he shouted at the crew.

Soaked and freezing, Max crumpled to the deck, knowing his last effort to stop the whales had failed.

39

The fog was becoming patchy. It opened in spots, then closed again. On the *Noah*'s bridge, Jesse and the others peered out hopefully.

"There she is!" Randolph cried and pointed.

Jesse caught a glimpse of the whaler's boat, a hundred yards off starboard. Drew grabbed the radio and talked into the handheld mike. "*Botany Bay*, this is the *Noah*. We know who you are and what you're doing. If you attempt to harm these whales —"

She covered the mike with her hand and turned to Randolph. "What do I say?"

"Tell them they'll be fired upon," Randolph said.

"You will be fired upon!" Drew threatened into the mike, then clicked it off and looked at Randolph again. "With what? We don't have anything to fire upon them."

"It's a good thing they don't know that," Randolph replied with a wink.

Meanwhile, Jesse looked down at the computer.

The two blips were together again! "They're right on top of them!"

"Take the helm!" Drew ordered.

Jesse grabbed it. He had never in his life steered a ship even half that size. "What do I do?"

"Just steer," Drew said. "It's easy."

Jesse held onto the wheel while Drew ran out onto the deck and aimed a flare pistol. *Foom!* A bright chartreuse flare burst out and sailed across the *Botany Bay*'s bow.

On the bridge, the radio crackled: "*Noah*, this is the *Botany Bay*. We are fishing for salmon. Please stay clear. *We can't see a thing in this fog.*"

Jesse knew they were bluffing. And he could up the ante considerably. He picked up the radio and switched to the emergency channel that all boats, including the *Botany Bay* could hear: "S.O.S. Coastal Marine Patrol. This is the *Noah*. There's been a collision. S.O.S!"

Randolph stared at him. "You serious?"

Jesse nodded.

Randolph took the helm. "Better let me steer."

Jesse ran out to the deck. Ahead he could see the *Botany Bay*. Someone was on the bow, aiming the harpoon cannon! It was John Wesley, Max's dad!

"Hey!" Jesse shouted.

John Wesley didn't look up. He was aiming . . . Squeezing the trigger . . .

Thwunk! The bow of the *Noah* rammed the

125

Botany Bay amidships. Everyone on both boats was thrown on impact! John Wesley went overboard.

And then everything seemed to stop.

The waves caused by the impact rippled away, leaving an eerie silence. The *Botany Bay* was listing slightly. People on both boats found their footing and stood up. Max stood up, and his eyes met Jesse's. They both looked down into the water. They could see Max's father a few feet below the surface.

A killer whale was closing in on him.

Jesse winced as Willy butted John Wesley with his snout. Either Willy would kill Wesley, or Wesley would drown.

"Willy, stop!" Jesse shouted.

Somehow Wesley managed to reach the surface. He shouted at Sanderson, who was standing on the deck of the *Botany Bay*, aiming a spear gun. "Shoot it! Now! Fire!"

Sanderson kept trying to aim, but he couldn't get a clear shot without the risk of hitting Wesley as well. Meanwhile, Willy turned tightly and headed for Wesley at top speed. Jesse was certain the impact would kill Max's father.

"Willy, no!" Max shouted. *Screeeeeek!* He ran his fingers along the hull of the *Botany Bay*.

At the very last second, Willy veered away, then circled Max's dad, eyeing him.

Jesse breathed a sigh of relief, but not for long.

Crack! The wooden hoist on the *Botany Bay* gave way! Still treading water, John Wesley looked up just in time to see it topple down on him. In a flash he was tangled in its net as it dragged him under.

40

John Wesley knew he was done for. He was caught in the net and sinking like a stone. He could feel the water pressure building on his eardrums and he swallowed involuntarily to equalize the pressure. The light from the surface was disappearing as he sank into the darkness.

He felt a strange kind of peace.

He'd always known he'd die at sea.

Maybe it was best this way.

Then he had a shock. A big brown eye was staring at him! It was that whale! It was swimming alongside as he sank.

Making sure I go down, huh? Wesley thought ruefully. *Guess you won after all.*

As if Willy had read his mind, he swam under the hoist, and nudged the whaler gently back to the surface.

41

Jesse and Randolph went out in the dinghy and helped Wesley out of the water. By the time they brought him back to the *Noah*, two coastal marine patrol boats had arrived. One boat pulled up next to the *Botany Bay*. The officers aboard appeared to be taking a great interest in the harpoon cannon.

Another coastal marine patrol officer boarded the *Noah* and approached Jesse, Randolph, and Drew.

"Is one of you Drew Halbert?" he asked.

"I am," Drew said.

"I have a message from your captain," the officer said. "You're fired."

The officer left and Drew turned to Jesse. "I knew you'd get me fired."

"Big deal," Randolph said with a smile. "He does that to me all the time."

On the other side of the deck, John Wesley huddled under a blanket and watched the coastal marine patrol officers go through the *Botany Bay*. Max joined him.

"Looks like a big, swimming cheeseburger saved your life, Dad," Max said.

His father turned to him. "Why'd he do it?"

"He thinks I'm family," Max said proudly.

John Wesley studied his son for a moment, then nodded. "You were right about them."

"Hey, no big deal." Max hugged his father. "You made a mistake. That's how we learn."

"And what am I supposed to do now?" John Wesley asked. "I'm a whaler. That's what I am."

"Not to me," Max replied. "You're my dad."

Across the deck, Jesse, Randolph, and Drew watched them.

"That's not what I would have done," Drew said under her breath.

"What do you mean?" Randolph asked.

"A guy tries to kill me, I wouldn't have saved him," Drew said. "I would have eaten him."

"Maybe Willy's just smarter than we are," Jesse said.

"Or more human," added Randolph.

Jesse looked over the side at Willy, who was swimming with Nicky. "He'll make a good father, don't you think?"

Postscript

Wearing wet suits, Jesse and Randolph lowered themselves off the dinghy and into the water. Max and Drew handed each of them a waterproof video camera. Jesse gave them a thumbs-up sign and plunged beneath the surface.

He hadn't gone far before Willy swam up to him and started to chatter happily. Jesse lowered his camera and patted his old friend on the snout. A second later Willy swam off and back to Nicky.

The two whales swam together, orbiting each other in a nose-to-nose dance until Nicky swam away. From her underside, a small black shape appeared. Nicky stopped, and pushed. An infant orca slid gracefully into the water, swimming right through the rosy cloud of his mother's blood.

Cameras rolling, Jesse and Randolph followed as Nicky gently nudged her baby to the surface, where he drew his first breath. The baby had those three black dots on his chest, just like Willy. He lingered for a moment on the surface, then plunged back into the water to explore a new world.

Drew had been taping the birth from the surface, using a third video camera. When she lowered it from her face, Max started to laugh.

"I like it, Drew," Jesse said with a grin as he pulled off his mask.

"What?" Drew asked.

"It brings out your eyes," Jesse said.

Drew wiped her eye. Her fingers came away black with soot that Jesse had rubbed around the camera's eyepiece.

"Well, *one* of your eyes, anyway," Jesse said.

Drew just smiled. "I guess I deserved that."

Randolph tapped Jesse on the shoulder, then pointed back at the two whales and their baby. "What are we going to call him?"

Jesse looked at Max. "What do you say?"

"Me?" Max was surprised Jesse had asked.

"Yeah, you," Jesse said.

Max didn't have to think about it for long. "I say we name him after his dad."

"I say we name him 'Max,'" Jesse said with a smile.

About the Author

Todd Strasser has written many award-winning novels for young and teenage readers. Among his best-known books are *Help! I'm Trapped in Obedience School* and *Girl Gives Birth to Own Prom Date*. He speaks frequently at schools about the craft of writing and conducts writing workshops for young people. He and his family live in a place near the water with their yellow Labrador retriever, Mac.